Famous

IN A SMALL TOWN

KYLIE SCOTT

NEW YORK TIMES BESTSELLING AUTHOR

Famous in a Small Town
Copyright © 2022 by Kylie Scott

Editor: Kelli Collins at Edit Me This
Copy Editor: Lisa Wolff
Formatter: Champagne Book Design
Photographer: Andrew M Gleason
Cover Designer: Regina Wamba

TP-ISBN: 978-0648457343

Playlist

"lovely" by Billie Eilish and Khalid

"Shake It Out" by Florence + The Machine

"A Case of You" by Joni Mitchell

"I Can't Feel My Face" by The Weeknd

"Hallelujah" by Jeff Buckley

"Stars" by Grace Potter and The Nocturnals

"Meet Me At Our Spot" by Willow, THE ANXIETY, and Taylor Cole

"Permission to Dance" by BTS

"You Right" by Doja Cat and The Weeknd

"You Send Me" by Aretha Franklin

Famous

IN A SMALL TOWN

Chapter One

MY NEW NEIGHBOR ARRIVED AT MIDNIGHT ON A Thursday. First came the moving truck, followed by a black SUV. Mrs. Cooper, the former owner of the house, passed away a while back. A damn shame. The woman was not only nice, but she made biscuits like you wouldn't believe. For years the grand old Victorian house sat empty at the end of the cul-de-sac. Not unusual for a small town. Few people wanted to move to the middle of nowhere in Northern California, no matter how picturesque it might be. While the house had been sold not long after listing, there'd been no sighting of the new owner until now.

Who the hell moved in the middle of the night? It seemed covert and suspicious. Like something a criminal or government agent would do. Maybe this just happened to be the time they arrived. But most people would stay at a hotel and wait for daylight. Surely.

The only things ever happening at midnight in Wildwood were: 1. Harry, the town drunk, performing Bob Dylan classics in the middle of Main Street. 2. Me, an insomniac, wandering aimlessly around my house. That was it. Everyone else in the whole wide world—or our corner of it—was fast asleep.

Half hidden behind a curtain, I watched the truck being unloaded. A full moon shone down through the pine trees as the moving men hauled stuff inside. The guy who drove the SUV went straight into the house. He was white and tall and wore a ball cap. That was about all I could see. Maybe he was setting the place up for his wife and family. Maybe he had a boyfriend. He couldn't possibly be single, heterosexual, under sixty, and emotionally mature. My luck just wasn't that good. Not that I intended to date again in this lifetime.

Whoever he was and whatever he was doing, it would all be known in due course. Such was the joy of small-town life.

Once the furniture was moved inside, things got a little dull. There's not much you can tell about people from their boxes.

I took the opportunity to once again check the locks on all my windows and doors. Then I made a cup of chamomile tea. Neither of these things helped me sleep, but the rituals were soothing. Mom always said I had a busy mind. I didn't necessarily think about anything useful, I just thought a lot. At night, I tended to think about books, bad memories, and ex-boyfriends. The last two were often one and the same. Along with a mixture of random embarrassing moments throughout my life just for fun.

As a child, I was the daydreamer who got busted humming in class when everyone else was concentrating. (Like anybody actually needed algebra. If you can work out the discount at a shoe sale, you're good to go. Then again, this attitude might explain why my life had gone approximately nowhere.)

I returned to the window just in time to see my mystery man reappear. The new neighbor strode out to the Range Rover and opened up the back. When he once more headed toward the house, the ball cap was gone and his shoulder-length hair was on display. In each hand he carried a guitar case.

I perked up. Musicians were cool. Unless he owned electric guitars and believed in turning the volume up to eleven. That could get old fast.

As he got closer to the house, the porch light hit him and . . . huh. Something about his profile tugged at a memory.

Guess he felt my gaze, because he turned toward my place. And whoa. His lips were a thin line, his jaw set to cranky, but none of it mattered—the man was beautiful. His high forehead and sharp cheekbones were nothing less than stunning. Though he really was strangely familiar.

Meanwhile, with only a lamp on behind me, I couldn't have been more than an outline. A shadowy person lurking in the dark. Great. Nothing like being spied on to make you feel welcome in your new neighborhood. So much better than a casserole or cookies.

Hold on. I knew where I recognized him from. Only it couldn't be, because that would be ridiculous. Absolutely fucking wild. Yet there he stood.

"Holy shit," I whispered.

My new neighbor was a goddamn rock star.

The Wildwood General Store opened at seven a.m. I was not a morning person, but installing the coffee machine had been my bright idea. And locals who rose early for work needed their caffeine fix. So I donned my uniform: a long-sleeve striped Henley, blue jeans, and black Chucks. Because comfort matters. Tied my brown hair up in a ponytail and got my butt into gear. Working in a small-town general store was never my dream. Which isn't to say I don't enjoy my work, but it's funny where life takes you. For instance, it took me all the way to Los Angeles and back again. And I learned my lesson: here is where I'd stay.

When I arrived at work, the first thing I did was remove the copy of *Rolling Stone* from the magazine rack. My neighbor might not be on the cover, but he'd probably be mentioned inside. There'd been plenty of articles about him over the last two years. Often about his band breaking up and his personal life going to hell in a handbasket. Imagine having strangers all over the world dissecting and discussing your life like it was nothing. And I now lived next to someone who was regularly in the gossip magazines. Weird.

As per my usual, I overthought the situation with my new neighbor. The conclusion I had reached was . . . if I were a world-famous rock star who'd bought a house in a small town in the middle of nowhere and moved in at midnight, it could only be for one reason: I wanted to be left the fuck alone.

Though I highly doubted that would happen. Hadn't I already been caught spying on the poor man? And I wouldn't be the last. Any new person in town became the center of attention, let alone someone famous.

The owner of the small general store, Linda, usually wandered in around nine. Her family had been around since the land the town stood on was taken from the local Native Americans. In fact, her great-great-grandfather had built the original wooden construction that housed the store. When it burned down about a century back in a forest fire (along with the brothel and a barber shop), it was replaced with this two-story stone building. Most of the wooden display cases and shelving dated back to those days. Of course, the line of silver fridges and freezers along the back wall did not.

We stocked a little bit of everything, from boxed mac and cheese to truffle oil (which, incidentally, went together to great effect). The shop aesthetic I was aiming for was a mix of new and old, with a dash of boho thrown in for good measure. Because while we were convenient, we were still in competition with the large supermarket and weekly farmers' market in the next town over. And the tourists who visited expected a certain ambience.

Linda liked to sit at the corner table with her pack of tarot cards and a pot of tea. She'd done a lot of living in the '60s. These days she just wanted to hang out in her family business and have everything be mellow and groovy. Her words, not mine. Which left me to manage things. Given my ever so carefully hidden control-freak tendencies, this was for the best. Her mishandling of the produce display one time still blew my mind. Gourds deserved more respect. And her efforts at tidying the book swap section I'd introduced were downright horrifying. Women's Fiction was not Romance. Everyone knows that.

Before Linda came Claude. He dropped off freshly baked goods several times a week. He'd been a pastry chef at a big hotel in Chicago. On the first day of his retirement, he realized he hated fishing, wasn't into hunting or hiking, and didn't know what to do with himself. Unlike my boss, relaxing was not Claude's thing. When he offered to keep the coffee shop section of the store's bakery case stocked, I said yes. Best decision ever, though my hips might disagree.

"Ani, taste this," he said, passing me his latest creation.

"Oh my God," I groaned when I could speak. Flaky pastry, sweet fruit, and all-around deliciousness. "Fried apple pie?"

The older dark-skinned man nodded.

"Amazing," I said around another bite.

Which, of course, was when the walkers burst in—three local women who actually looked good in yoga pants. They could keep their husbands and children. But for their butts, I felt envy. Most mornings they were out there, marching up and down Main Street, while I was here, shoving food in my face like a champion.

"You have a new neighbor," accused the first walker.

"Why didn't you tell us?" asked the second.

The third walker just looked at me with judgment and amazing brows. I wondered where she got them done.

"Someone finally moved into old Mrs. Cooper's place?" Claude leaned against the wooden counter, sipping his latte. He might be a late addition to Wildwood, but it didn't take him long to be tuned into local gossip. "Hadn't even heard it was sold."

"A few years back," I said. "But I know nothing about it."

The first walker sighed, heavily disappointed in my life choices. *You and me both, lady.*

While the second said, "I better get home, make one of my boysenberry pies to take over."

"But I was going to take pie!"

"You can never have too much pie." Claude smiled and waved goodbye on his way out the door.

"That's true," I agreed quickly. Because the last thing we needed was a girl fight over pie.

I guess the walkers had silently decided to rush home and

start baking, because without another word, the pack about-faced and left.

Of course, I knew their names. But two of them were such assholes to me back in high school that I refused to validate them, and the third was guilty by association. Hooray for being petty.

Childhood bullying and media expectations were why I now sought to embrace my mediocrity. My height and weight and hair are all quite ordinary, and that's fine. There are more important things. Like not spending your whole damn life at war with yourself. I have solid friends, a job that I like, a stack of excellent books waiting to be read on my bedside table, boxed mac and cheese in the pantry, and a bottle of vodka in the freezer. Life was good. Once I managed to get a decent night's sleep, it would be perfect.

That was when he strode in. The rock star.

The man was dressed in blue jeans, boots, a faded gray tee, and the ball cap. He clearly didn't want to draw attention to himself. Which was mission impossible, if you ask me. With his head down, he grabbed a basket and got busy. Despite the skulking, he moved with purpose. He was sure of himself and his place in the world. Imagine having that kind of confidence. I was still trying to get my shit together at thirty. And there he was at thirty-seven, having fronted a world-famous band and been happily married to a talented musician. Only to then live through losing both of those things. How devastating.

I watched him on the sly while making another coffee. There was a lot to see and admire. Like the way his sleeves stretched just so around his biceps. The width of his shoulders and breadth of his chest. He was a walking, talking teenage dream.

Luckily, I knew better than to crush on someone so out of my league. Though no wonder the media loved him and fans flocked to hear him play. Along with being a talented musician, he was a visual delight.

The truth of it is, big brawny men appeal to my lizard brain. It's a terrible thing.

He stopped in front of the local arts and crafts section, perusing the pottery mugs, wooden bowls, and jewelry made out of fancy old silver spoons and forks. A macramé guitar strap in particular held his attention. My personal favorite item was a painting of redwoods after a rainstorm. One day it would be mine. In the meantime, I was happily addicted to the handmade soaps, small-batch teas, and artisan chocolates. Because there's no shortage of cool creators in Nor Cal.

I had so many questions for the rock star. Like, why move here? Given everything he'd been through, I could understand the need to disappear. What with his wife dying and his band breaking up. But why not hide out on a tropical island? I was pasty and couldn't tan. I was also mildly allergic to mosquitos. Their bites made me blotchy. However, I still would have been on the first flight out of here. With a margarita in my hand, I'd happily live out the rest of my days in a grass hut. As long as it had a functioning bathroom. Every woman has her limits.

He placed his shopping basket on the big old wooden counter. Stubble lined his jaw and the brim of his cap hid the upper half of his face. There was a white tan line on his ring finger. Like he'd only just removed his wedding ring. Another reminder that he'd been to hell and back. What he needed was for someone to show him some consideration. To be kind to him. And that I could do.

I set down the coffee in its recyclable cup on the counter. My hand only shook a little, thank goodness. "For you."

Nothing from him.

"I'm your new neighbor."

"You were the one watching last night." His voice was deep, a little rough, and kind of accusing. "In that little cabin next door."

"Yes."

"You do that sort of thing often . . . spying on people?"

Ouch. Previous me was a dreadful snoop, and I was both embarrassed and appalled by her behavior. But I'd evolved in the last eight or so hours. While I'd hoped my apology could go unspoken, it clearly couldn't. "It won't happen again. Sorry."

After a moment, he picked up the coffee and took a sip. All without meeting my gaze. Eye contact was apparently out of the question.

"Do you take cream or sugar?" I asked.

"No. This is fine. Thanks." No wonder he was a singer. Even those clipped and cranky words could have charmed the birds down from the trees. His voice was low and smooth and just lovely.

Into a cardboard box went his loaf of bread, jars of peanut better and strawberry jelly, coffee, a six-pack of beer, and some ramen noodles. Hunger must have driven him out into the open. Guess he usually had someone cook for him. Live-in staff was likely standard for a Hollywood Hills mansion. The man was in for a change of pace.

"We stock all of your basics," I said. "But if you ever want a bigger shop, there's a good-size market in the town about half an hour down the road. You probably drove past it on your way here."

He grunted.

I totaled his purchases and he paid with a black Amex. Something I'd heard about, but never actually seen.

As he was gathering his things, Linda floated in on a wave of rose-hip oil. It was her beauty secret. Great for keeping your skin hydrated. The medicinal marijuana she indulged in helped keep her calm and thus avoid wrinkles. And it worked. She really did look great for her age. Her red suede fringed bag bumped against her side with each step, her worn cowboy boots tapping against the wooden floor. I could never hope to be as cool and fun as Linda. This was a fact.

"Mercury is in retrograde again, Ani," she exclaimed, brandishing her cell. "Everything is chaos."

"Okay," I said. "I'm with a customer right now, but—"

"I accidentally deleted the most important email."

"Did you look in the trash?"

Her brows went up.

"Remember how I showed you those other files on your phone where emails hide sometimes?"

Linda must have finally realized that a customer was present. Because she froze and pasted on a smile. "Oh, hello. Welcome to the Wildwood General Store."

He tipped his chin. "Ma'am."

"Are you new in town or just passing through?"

The man opened his mouth and then stalled. Nothing came out.

"Goodness," she said, recognition lighting her gaze. "You

look exactly like that singer from that rock band. You know the one I mean. What was his name?"

His jaw shifted nervously as he stared at the floor. Guess I was right about him wanting to hide. But given that his band had been topping the charts for the last decade, he really should be better at dealing with people recognizing him.

"Oh, you mean Garrett from The Dead Heart." I fake smiled. "Yeah. He does look a little like him, doesn't he?"

Linda snapped her fingers. "Yes. That's who I mean. I should remember—you played that last album of theirs day and night for a while there."

"I don't recall that," lied my lying tongue.

"Oh, good Lord. I was hearing those songs in my sleep."

I wrinkled my nose. "They were probably playing it over at the bar and you heard it there. I wasn't . . . I mean, it was a good album, but . . ."

"Didn't you even have a picture of him on your phone?"

Heat crept up my neck. "No."

Little wonder Garrett hadn't gone into acting. Every thought he had seemed to cross his face. And amusement dominated. So not helpful. Could he not try to work with me here? Did he not see that I was trying to help him?

Linda was gossip central in Wildwood. She made it her business to know everything about everyone. She sat at her corner table and told everyone the latest news as they walked in the door. And if Linda believed the new man in town was a nobody, who only looked like a famous somebody, then his cover might not be blown for days or weeks.

"She's right, though," I said. "You could almost be a look-alike. Bet you'd win competitions and everything."

11

Garrett just blinked.

"It's amazing." Linda shook her head. "He really is similar."

"They say everyone has a doppelganger, right?" I asked. "That there's someone out there who looks exactly the same as you."

"That's true." Linda frowned. "It's lucky you're not him. The problems he's had these last few years. Makes you just want to give him a big ol' hug. Maybe I should give you one instead!"

Garrett's eyes went as wide as the moon.

"Oh, I don't think touching is necessary," I said. "Ever."

"Your generation has no appreciation for the comfort of skin on skin. Simply connecting with another person." Linda smiled and made her way toward her corner table. "Would you be so kind as to make me a pot of tea, Ani?"

"Of course." I turned back to the bewildered rock star. "Have a nice day, sir."

"Uh, thanks," he said after a moment.

Then I mouthed, "Run."

It wouldn't take long for Linda to regroup. Then she'd want to hear his life story. In fact, she would demand it. And the woman could talk for days.

The rock star reached for his groceries, strong hands gripping the sides of the box. Then he gave me one last confused look. It was almost as if he wanted to say something. But instead, he just left.

How about that. I'd met one of my heroes and lust objects. Somewhat humiliating, with a side order of exciting. Maybe he'd run back to Los Angeles, now that he realized hiding out here wouldn't be so easy after all. At least I'd gotten to meet him. Just went to show, sordid dreams could come true. #blessed

Chapter Two

THE REST OF THE DAY WENT MUCH THE SAME AS ALWAYS. Apart from the myriad questions about my new neighbor. To which I claimed ignorance on all counts. It was my memory of the photos they'd taken of him leaving his wife's funeral that made me so determined to protect the man. How broken and lost he'd looked. That had resonated with me for various reasons.

After the funeral, he'd pretty much disappeared from public life. And while a case could be made that I was lying my little heart out to the population of Wildwood, I was also protecting his privacy. Once news of his superstar status broke, I'd pretend to be as shocked as the rest of the town. What a fraud. Though it was for a good cause.

The knock on my door came just after nine p.m. And there stood my neighbor with a scowl on his handsome face. I wasn't used to being around beautiful people. He made me break out in a nervous sweat. I was sure to blurt out something breathtakingly stupid any moment now. How could anyone be coherent when confronted with such perfection?

Also, his timing was awesome. If only every rock 'n' roll idol could see me with a messy bun, in a tank top and sleep shorts. This was why having a front door with a glass panel was a bad idea. But it was original, with colored glass in a pretty pattern. I couldn't bring myself to replace it, despite the security risk.

After pulling the hair tie out of my bun, I slid back the deadbolt and the security chain before unlocking the door with a strained smile. Holding my hair down over the old scar on my neck as subtly as can be. "Garrett. Hi."

"What do you want?" he asked, tone curious.

"Huh?"

"You heard me."

I cocked my head. "You knocked on my door. Which would suggest that it's you who wants something."

"I meant for covering for me today at the store." He shoved his hands in his front jeans pockets. "What do you want?"

"What?" I asked. "Like payment?"

"You want me to sign some stuff or take a selfie with you or what?"

"Wow. Is that how things usually work in your world?"

He scowled and loomed over me. Though even that was disgustingly attractive. The man had to be well over six feet tall. I was average height and weight, and I still almost felt dainty beside him. He clearly wasn't in a smiling mood, which made me wonder what his happiness levels were before his wife's death. Not that it was any of my business. I'd never come close to finding a life partner, let alone experiencing the pain of losing one. I kept the pity off my face, however. Something told me he would not appreciate the sentiment.

"Not saying that we're more pure or anything around these parts," I said. "But we at least don't expect something in return when helping someone out."

He grunted. And kept right on waiting for my list of demands, apparently.

"Okay then. Thanks for the offer, but my show is on and I don't want anything from you. Have a nice night."

Before I could shut the door in his face, his big-ass hand rose to hold it open. "Wait a minute. Last night you were all but hanging out your window watching me—"

"I wasn't hanging out of anything," I scoffed. "And I apologized for that. You make me sound like some deranged stalker. But who wouldn't be curious about a new neighbor? I get that it's probably an issue for you. People not respecting your boundaries and so on. But did it ever occur to you that maybe you're being a little bit oversensitive?"

"Then today it seemed like you were sort of trying to have my back by not saying who I was," he said, carrying on as if I hadn't spoken.

"There was no 'sort of' about it, I totally had your back. You're welcome," I said. "Though you should enjoy it while you can. Word will get around about you eventually."

The furrows upon his handsome brow were beyond count.

"You might have been better off trying to hide in a big city, with a face as famous as yours . . ."

He licked his lips, like he was about to say something,

only nothing came out. A perplexed expression crossed his face. Finally he confessed, "People have been leaving food at my door all day."

"You didn't answer when they knocked?" I asked, amused.

He shrugged.

"Did you actually hide behind a couch or—"

"No. Of course not. I just didn't answer."

"You can relax. It's not a coordinated attack. They're just welcoming you to town. And yeah, maybe they're a little curious about you. But there's nothing particularly nefarious going on." I smiled. "Though if you opened the door, one of them would have recognized you. Famous people aren't the norm around here. You likely won't stay anonymous for long. Unless you're willing to become a shut-in for the rest of your life, like Miss Havisham."

"Who?"

"She's a character in a book," I explained. "Look on the bright side: with all that food you won't have to live on peanut-butter-and-jelly sandwiches and ramen noodles. That's a plus, right?"

He wasn't convinced.

"Don't they welcome people to the neighborhood in Beverly Hills?"

"I wouldn't know," he said. "Never lived there."

Then his gaze wandered down me and paused on my chest, before darting away. No bra. A veritable booby trap. But he was the one who knocked on my door. I would feel no shame. I refused to. Though I did immediately cross my arms over my chest—for nipple-related reasons.

He cleared his throat. "I came here to get some peace."

"When you finish the food, you can give the dishes to me and I'll return them to their owners. That should buy you a little more time."

"Thanks." He paused. "I didn't catch your name."

"Do you need to know my name?"

"Is everything always this hard with you?"

I pondered the question. "No. Not everything. But you put me on the defensive. I think it's that line between your brows when you look at me. It's so judgy."

He snorted. "But you like my band."

"I like a lot of bands."

He almost smiled. It was close.

Approximately a million questions sat on the tip of my tongue. But I didn't ask even one. "My name is Ani."

"Ani." He nodded. "Nice to meet you."

"Welcome to Wildwood, Garrett."

Without another word, he turned and headed for home. There was something wary about the set of his shoulders as he disappeared off into the darkness. Made me wonder if he actually enjoyed being on his own, in that big old house. But, the truth is, you could surround yourself with people and still be alone.

Work began the next day on a fence around his yard. A tall stone one with a decorative iron gate and inserts. There were even spikes on the top. It went up faster than I thought possible. Next came the van with a security company logo on the side. The rock star made himself a veritable stronghold on the edge of our small town.

"Oh, that is such bullshit."

"You sit down now, Maria, or I'll be taking a point off your team." Heather banged her gavel against the table. "The paper says Stevie Nicks."

"Everyone knows the first woman ever inducted into the hall of fame was Aretha Franklin." Maria took a pull on her beer. "This is ridiculous. Stevie was the first woman to be inducted twice. Get your facts straight."

"She's right, Heather," said Harry, who sat at the bar. When he wasn't inebriated and performing at midnight on Main Street, his musical knowledge was legendary. "Aretha Franklin was first."

Heather just rubbed her temple.

Trivia nights at the bar often got heated. The week before, a passionate debate involving much finger pointing broke out over which year construction started on the Empire State Building. It was 1930, by the way.

The local population was an interesting mix. It consisted of free-loving hippies, serious-faced flannel-wearing types, and assorted others. And despite protestations from some regarding world peace, a competitive streak ran through the town a mile wide. That's why the county sheriff banned any betting on pool games. Too many fistfights. Bingo was also right out. The last time it had been played, there'd been a veritable bloodbath.

I sat at a table with my good friends, who just so happened to be my trivia night group. We called ourselves The Matriarchy Monsters and we often won trivia night.

The bar was what you'd expect. Lots of wood and the occasional dead animal head. But the food was good and the drinks reasonably priced. It was comfortable. It was ours.

"How's that neighbor of yours?" Cézanne was a Black

woman who owned a local winery. She had natural hair, a gorgeous smile, and excellent taste in cheese. Because cheese is life.

"I have no idea," I said, nursing my cider. "Still hiding behind his walls. Various contractors have come and gone, but he remains concealed."

"It should be illegal to come to town and refuse to take part in our tomfoolery." Maria was a schoolteacher and the brains of our operation. Her knowledge of trivia was immense. And her olive skin was tanned to perfection, thanks to recently holidaying in Hawaii with her girlfriend. "We should storm the fortress."

That's what the locals had taken to calling the rock star's abode. The fortress. Fair enough, given the fence and other security measures he'd installed. But still his identity remained unknown.

It had been almost a week since his one and only appearance at the general store. Vehicles often came and went, but the owner of the house remained unseen. Not that I spied on him or anything. God forbid. And while I felt guilty about withholding information from my friends, I still couldn't bring myself to tell them. Like I'd be betraying him or something.

I smiled. "You're going to force him to socialize?"

"We'll make him host a potluck at his place," said Cézanne.

"That would strike fear into the heart of any man." I popped another garlic fry in my mouth. Because it was important to eat your vegetables.

"That's a great idea," enthused Claude from the next table. "I could make my chili."

Maria frowned. "Claude. No. Your sourdough is the best I've ever tasted. Chili is just not your calling."

"I've been working on it. Your mother's helping me. She's teaching me the family recipe."

"For fuck's sake, Mama," muttered Maria, shaking her head.

Cézanne grinned. "I think it's great that Claude and your mom are dating."

"Whatever makes them happy," said Maria with a pained sigh.

Her father passed away eight years ago from a heart attack. Claude had been asking her mother out to dinner repeatedly for the past few years. But up until recently, the answer was always, "Not yet. Ask me again next month." Moving on from over thirty years of marriage had to be hard. Change in general wasn't always easy to embrace.

Take the rock star. His wife, Grace, had been gone for two years before he took off his wedding ring. And then hid himself away in our town. The man made no sense. Not that I was going to think about him, because thinking about him was a waste of time. I couldn't even have naked thoughts about him in private anymore. It was just too weird. They always say never meet your heroes in real life. And they are right.

Uncanny how a song by his deceased wife came on the jukebox just then. She purred and growled about what a bitch love could be. Such an amazing voice. And of course she'd been stunning. I pitied the person who tried to displace her in his heart.

"I'll never forget the time I saw her in concert," said Maria.

Cézanne pouted. "You're damn lucky. I always wanted to see Grace perform, but I kept putting it off and now it's too late."

"She was wild. It was at a festival and The Dead Heart were playing too," continued Maria. "They did a song together, and man . . . those two had chemistry like you wouldn't believe."

Heather banged her gavel. "The Matriarchy Monsters have won. Again."

We jumped to our feet to celebrate, while our competitors booed. It was mostly good-natured. Mostly.

"Lucky you knew about the Whipple Tickle." Maria tapped her bottle of beer against my cider before turning to Cézanne with a smile. "And you, with your unexpected yet delightful knowledge of sperm whales. Excellent work."

"It was a team effort, as always," said Cézanne.

"And they call it trivia." I shrugged. "How do other people even sleep at night without knowing this random shit? Do they know what they're missing?"

"The Matriarchy Monsters suck!" yelled someone by the bar.

I gave them my queenly wave. The one I learned from watching a royal wedding with Mom as a child. "Maria, it's your turn to take home the winner's growler. Enjoy it in good health. I'm out of here, ladies."

"Me too," said Maria. "I promised Danielle I'd be home at a decent hour."

We exchanged hugs, then I headed out to my vehicle. My beloved old Chevy truck that I'd owned since high school. Puddles filled the parking lot and gray clouds hung low overhead. Given better weather, I could have walked home. Not that I tended to wander around after dark, because that made me nervous as heck. But the actual town of Wildwood was not that big. Just a grid consisting of Main Street, Church Street, and School Street. Crossed with River Street, Hill Street, and Oak Lane. Inventive street names were not our forte. But at least it made it hard to get lost.

Showing that my winning streak was holding strong, my old Chevy started on the third try. A total win.

I was climbing out of the truck back home in my driveway when a stranger walked up to me. It was like he appeared out of nowhere, this giant shadow person. My heart hammered as I fumbled in my purse for the can of mace. Why the hell the outside sensor light hadn't come on, I had no idea. Random attack squirrels could set it off, but not people?

"Thank God you're here. This is an emergency," the large man said. Then he saw the expression on my face and took a step back. "Shit. Sorry. I didn't mean to . . . I'm from next door. I was wondering if you had a corkscrew."

My special friend who lived in the next town over would be so disappointed by my failure to spring into action when approached by a vaguely threatening stranger in the dark. When I'd moved back to town, we'd met through his self-defense course. Maybe I needed a refresher in actual defense strategies, as opposed to just an occasional visit to his bedroom.

I did my best to calm my breathing. "Next door?"

"Garrett's place." He waved a bottle of wine in the general direction of my neighbor's house. "I brought up a case of this vintage red and the idiot doesn't own a corkscrew."

"Oh."

And that's when it hit me. The exceedingly tall, blond, bearded, tattooed man was the lead guitarist from The Dead Heart. Whoa. Guess I should have foreseen the possibility of more famous people in my future. However, it stunned me just the same.

"I'm hoping you have one," he said with a warm smile, after

I'd only been staring at him for a full minute. He just seemed to take my reaction in stride, however. "A corkscrew, that is."

"Sure. Yes." I blinked. It took a moment to get my brain back on line. "Let me just . . ."

Smith waited at the door while I fussed with the keys, then rushed into the kitchen. Any wine I drank usually had a screw top. But of course, rock stars drank cases of expensive vintage wine. The bottle he was holding probably cost more than my whole world. He made no move to enter my place, which was good. Strange men in my space didn't work well for me.

At last, I found it—ever so slightly rusted and hidden at the back of my junk drawer. If they wanted designer barware, they'd come to the wrong house.

"Here you go." I smiled.

"You should come over for a drink. Have a glass with us."

"Um. I don't know if that's a good idea."

He cocked his head. "Why not?"

"Garrett and I sort of got off to a rocky start and . . . yeah, I'm not sure he actually likes me."

"See now, there's your mistake." He leaned closer and spoke in a low and slow voice like he was sharing a secret. There was a gentleness to the big man that was appealing. Along with the masculine prettiness, of course. "Garrett doesn't actually like anyone."

"Huh."

"He used to be fine, but the last few years . . ."

I raised my brows. "Right."

"So you'll come? Great," he said, offering me his hand. "The grass is a little slippery from the rain. Let me help you out."

While I probably should have said no, I didn't have it in

23

me to turn him down. Smith was genuinely charming and I was curious. I wanted to know what overpriced vintage red wine tasted like. And it's not like I'd be given the opportunity to hang out with rock stars again anytime soon. I may have had a small passing interest in seeing *him* again. But that was just me being neighborly.

"I forgot to introduce myself," he said, his grip on my hand firm but gentle. "I'm Smith."

"Ah, yeah. I know. I'm Ani."

"I know you are. He said you were a fan."

I wrinkled my nose. "Wait. Garrett talked about me?"

Smith grinned and led me out into the night.

Chapter Three

"A NI," HE SAID, VOICE DEVOID OF EMOTION.

"Hi, Garrett. How are you?"

The man sat in a big old black leather wingback chair with a guitar in his lap. And he did not look happy. How you could be unhappy living in a house with a turret, I had no idea. However, the scowl on his handsome face dominated the room. This is the problem with having a celebrity crush. For as long as they're out there in the big wide world somewhere, being unattainable, it's fine. But when they move in next door, things get complicated.

Though I had to admit he'd brought the old Cooper house back to life. A mixture of modern and vintage furniture in black and gray with pops of sky blue. Lots of velvet and leather and wood, which suited the place. The front parlor had been freshly painted the color of a storm cloud and was full of comfy chairs and sofas. More guitars waited on a stand in the corner and a fire burned low in the fireplace. There were no pictures anywhere, though. A veritable wall of vinyl and a killer turntable. But no photos. Which was odd.

And if I could just be cool and not stare at him, that would be great.

"We have a corkscrew and a guest," announced Smith, opening the wine and filling up the waiting glasses. "You take this one, Ani."

"Thank you." I accepted the drink from the gentle giant and took the seat farthest from the lord of the manor. "Looks like you're all moved in."

"Don't be too impressed," said Smith. "He paid people to unpack and do all this for him."

"Well, the house looks great. The furniture is perfect."

"Yeah. Grace had amazing style," said Smith with a soft smile.

Garrett's frown escalated alarmingly at the mention of his deceased wife's name.

"Buying this place was her idea for their retirement. She actually chose the—"

"That's enough," said Garrett.

Smith frowned and grabbed another glass off the cool old silver-and-glass bar cart. "Let's talk about something else, shall we?"

"You have a bar cart but no corkscrew?" I asked.

Garrett's gaze stayed glued to the guitar strings. "I don't drink wine."

"Heathen," mumbled Smith.

"Maybe I should go." I uncrossed my legs. On a scale of one to ten for awkwardness, tonight was sitting at a solid eleven. "Let you two visit in peace."

Smith poured his drink in silence. But the look he gave his friend was weighty.

"If you don't at least drink his fine wine first, you'll hurt his feelings," said Garrett, eventually.

"That's true. I'm much more delicate than I look." Smith raised his glass. "A toast to new friends."

Garrett and I both raised our glasses and drank. I tried to savor the experience, but the atmosphere was against me.

"You can really taste the caramel," enthused Smith. The man might look like a Viking, but apparently he had a fine palate. "And that hint of nuts it's got going on."

I smiled and took another sip. "It's lovely."

Garrett set aside his glass without comment. "Can I have a beer now?"

"Yes, I will fetch your boorish ass a beer. Don't know why I bother. You can bring a whore to culture, but you can't make him drink," mumbled Smith as he wandered out of the room.

The moment we were alone, I leaned forward and said, "It really is okay if you'd rather I leave."

"If you go, Smith will lecture me for the rest of the damn night. You have to stay now."

"Wow."

"What?"

"Nothing. Just basking in the warmth of your welcome." I made myself comfortable in the chair, nursing my glass of wine. And yay me for managing to look at him directly without spontaneously orgasming or blushing or any of that nonsense. "Let me guess, you think I'm going to run to the media and sell them juicy tales about you. Am I right, Garrett?"

His gaze was flat and unfriendly.

"You are sadly predictable, neighbor."

"I should just start trusting strangers now?"

"Notice the lack of locals stopping by to get a look at the new rock star in town?"

His jaw shifted. "You haven't told anyone."

"No. I haven't. Though I do feel weird withholding it from my friends. But I get that it's important to you to remain anonymous."

For a long moment, he just studied me, then he gave me a begrudging, "Thank you."

"You're welcome."

"Hey, everybody's getting along," said Smith, returning with a bottle of beer. "That's great."

"So great." I smiled. "And this wine is delicious."

Which was when a whole lot of commotion entered the room. Nails scrambled for purchase against the polished wooden floor. Then a deep, mighty "woof" was heard. A dog that was approximately the size of a horse bounded into the parlor and rushed straight at Garrett.

"Gene," said Garrett, holding onto the guitar with one hand while attempting to hold back the dog with the other. "You woke up, huh? How about you don't . . . okay. That's enough."

Once the Great Dane had managed to cover the man's face in dog spit via his large and long pink tongue, he about-faced to check out the rest of the room. His whole body vibrated with excitement, his tail wagging double time. That's when he spied me. I could see the adoration come to life in his eyes. The intent for us to be together for all time, or at least tonight, was clear as day.

"Oh no," was all I managed before he bounded across the

room at me. Then, well over a hundred pounds of excited canine made himself at home in my lap. Lucky for both of us, I managed to hold my glass of wine out to the side in time. "Hey there, puppy."

"Gene. Shit." Garrett appeared at my side and grabbed hold of the dog's collar. "C'mon, get down. You're going to crush her."

With a huff of disappointment, the dog obeyed. But he didn't go far. Paws back on the rug, he leaned against my legs and would go no farther. I ran my hand over his head, the short, soft fur like velvet beneath my palm. The doggo was a tactile delight. He was dark gray, apart from the white around his muzzle. And his collar was thick leather in that same sky blue with silver studs. Very cool.

"Is he always this friendly?" I asked.

A grunt from Garrett.

"No. Not usually. He's started getting confused sometimes, poor old boy," said Smith. "You're female and hanging out with Garrett, so he probably thinks you're Grace."

A flash of pain crossed Garrett's face. There and gone in an instant.

"She got him when he was a puppy and actually fit in her lap," continued Smith. "Didn't have the heart to stop him from doing it as he got bigger and bigger. You wouldn't believe how much fun it is having a dog this size on a tour bus or a private jet. But Grace insisted."

I waited for Garrett to go off again, but he didn't scold Smith for talking about his wife this time. He just headed for the bar cart and poured himself a scotch. A whole lot of scotch. Guess beer wasn't sufficient for tonight's reunion after all.

"Let me guess," I said, my gaze on the doggo. "Gene for Gene Simmons from Kiss on account of the ridiculously long tongue?"

Smith smiled, delighted. "You got it in one."

"My dad is a fan."

From the mighty collection of albums, Garrett selected one and put it on the turntable. The sound of a woman's voice soon filled the room. Then he sat back down. An interesting choice. I'd have expected him to go for more testosterone-fueled music. Some classic hair rock or early punk perhaps. But this sweet voice accompanied by an acoustic guitar was a pleasant surprise.

So this was how rock stars lived. This was how the rich and the famous spent their downtime. They hung out together, listened to great music, and drank expensive liquor. I could now officially say I'd been there and done that. Hanging-out wise.

"How many fingers of scotch is that?" asked Smith. "Four hands?"

"If you're going to insist on talking about her, I'm going to need it." Garrett set his ankle on the knee of his other leg. His feet were both bare and sizeable. They were also very clean, thank goodness. He set his head against the back of the chair and stared up at the ceiling, obviously lost in thought. "She loved this album."

"Yeah," said Smith. "Grace was a big Joni Mitchell fan."

Garrett flinched at the name, but again said nothing. It was as if Smith was dabbling in exposure therapy. And it actually seemed to be working.

I drank some wine and patted the puppy.

Smith watched his friend for a moment before turning back to me with a pained sort of smile. "Tell me about this town of yours, Ani."

"Ah, Wildwood is great. If you're into trees and mountains and mist and such," I said. "We have the general store, where I work. A bar and grill that has a nice seasonal menu along with the basics. And there's a great winery just down the road that does a charcuterie board like you wouldn't believe."

Smith nodded and waited for more.

"That's about it."

His brows rose in surprise. "It really is a small town then, huh?"

"Well, we also have a church, a gas station, post office, bank, a hardware, and a health clinic. There's also a vet who has an office just outside of town and a lady who converted her garage into a hair salon. We lost the diner about four years back when Eileen retired to San Diego. But the drugstore, pizzeria, mystic tarot card reader/crystal place, and the antique shop all closed down in the last year or two. The ice cream parlor didn't open this summer, which was sad. Times have been tough," I said. "This asshole inherited a bunch of buildings on Main Street and basically tripled the rent, making it impossible for people to stay in business. Though the inn is still going strong. They get the hunting, hiking, and fishing types who come through who don't want to camp."

"I see," I said Smith. "Garrett, what the hell are you going to do out here on your own?"

His friend drank like it was his life's calling. God help his liver.

Smith stared into his wine for a moment. "When you hid out in that apartment in New York for months on end, I understood. You needed time. Then you moved to the French chateau. Though really it was just a half-built crumbling old castle with

31

basic amenities. But it was sort of cool, and you could enjoy the quiet and maybe write some songs and sort yourself out. It seemed like a step in the right direction.

"But then you disappeared into the wilds of New Zealand. I was more than a little fucking worried about you backpacking on those trails alone, until I found out they don't actually have bears or cougars there. Just those weird little birds with long beaks that don't fly. But you were reasonably safe so long as you didn't walk off a cliff or try to fight any orcs. Finally you tell me that you're coming home. And the relief I felt, man. You have no idea. Only you don't come home, you come here instead."

Garrett sighed. "Take Gene back to L.A. with you when you go, would you?"

"He's your fucking dog now, and you're going to start looking after him," said Smith. While his voice stayed remarkably calm, the resolve was clear to all. "I know he reminds you of her, but hell . . . apparently everything does. Grace told me to give you a year. One year to mourn her before it was time for you to get your shit together and move on. You've had two."

Garrett's nostrils flared like that of some pissed-off stallion.

And maybe if I sat statue still they'd forget I was there. Because holy shit was this a personal conversation to be having in front of a veritable stranger.

"She asked me to look after you," said Smith. "And I gave her my word that I would. It's time for you to stop running and hiding and start living again."

Garrett's whole body had gone rigid. "Not your choice to make."

I set aside my wine. "And this is where I leave you guys to it."

"Actually, this next bit concerns you," said Smith.

"What?" I asked, incredulous.

Garrett screwed up his face. "How?"

"Glad you asked. It's actually the reason I invited your charming new neighbor to join us this evening." Smith let out a breath. "Garrett, you're going to get back out there and start living your life again. See your friends and start dating."

Garrett's heavy brows arched high. Then he asked with great disdain, "Dating?"

"Yes."

I raised my hand.

Smith cocked his head. "Ani?"

"Sorry to interrupt again. But what part of this involves me, exactly?"

"The dating part," said Smith in that same no-nonsense tone. "Do you know that within the first hour of my being here, Garrett looked out the window in the direction of your house no less than four times?"

"I was checking on the weather," grouched Garrett.

Smith took a sip of wine. "Liar."

"And making sure she wasn't watching me."

"Like you were watching *her*, because that would be . . . what exactly?"

Garrett's mouth slammed shut.

"Okay," I said. "I'm pretty sure the watching-my-place has more to do with his various neuroses than anything to do with actually liking me. But I feel like now is a good time to tell you that I don't date. Haven't done so for years, and I have no intention of starting again."

An expression of much relief passed over Garrett's face. Which was somewhat insulting. But whatever.

Smith frowned.

"Not that your friend here isn't a singular delight," I said. "But yeah, not a chance."

"Hmm." Smith swirled his wine around in the glass and thought deep thoughts. "May I ask why you don't date?"

"It's personal."

"You're amongst friends."

"It's deeply personal, and we actually only just met."

"Okay." Smith skewed his lips to one side. "So what, you don't find him attractive?"

Garrett looked to Heaven, but there was no help forthcoming. Then he turned to me and his gaze was . . . cranky but curious.

I downed the remaining half of my wine. For reasons. "He's a very attractive man, as I'm sure he well knows."

"Oh. Got it. You think he's egotistical." Smith grabbed the bottle and reached over to refill my glass.

"I didn't say that."

Smith nodded contemplatively. "I mean, I can kind of see where you're coming from."

"I repeat, I did not say that."

"Yeah, but you kind of inferred it," said Garrett with a vaguely malicious sort of glee. What a jerk.

"You really did," agreed Smith. "Though you also put the word *very* in front of *attractive*. So it's not all bad news, man."

Give me strength.

Smith clicked his fingers like he'd solved the puzzle. "Is he not rich enough for you? Is that it?"

Garrett scoffed. Talk about ego.

I just shook my head.

"Fine. Your charming neighbor is not available. We're going to need a backup plan." Smith shrugged and shoved a hand through his short blond hair. "Let me think. What about that nice production assistant who worked on the last album . . . what was her name . . . Savannah. That's it. She drove an awesome Impala. Huge backseat. Or there was Nicole from the lighting crew. You remember, she had gray hair. Very cute. Or Janis from the front desk at the record company. Lovely lady. And so flexible. Did you know she teaches yoga in her spare time?"

Garrett downed more of the scotch.

"Then there's the supermodels from that video we shot in Santa Monica. Nevena and Kista." Smith smiled wistfully at the memory. "Kista has a PhD in microbiology. Fascinating woman. And Nevena is working on her first romance novel, I believe. I wonder how she's doing with that."

"You're just listing off women you've slept with," said Garrett with his usual frown.

"And your point is? I have excellent taste in women," said Smith. "You'd be lucky to date any one of them. Though Nevena and Kista are actually an established couple looking to become a throuple. Best to keep that in mind if you give them a call."

Garrett sighed.

Smith turned to me with a shrug. "They really were all great. I just wasn't ready to settle down yet. And it's very hard to keep a long-term relationship going when you're on the road all the time. You know what it's like."

"Um," I said with much wisdom. "Not really."

He gave me a wink.

"The answer is no." Garrett shook his head. "All of them are probably located in L.A. and they're tied to the industry in one way or another. I already told you, I'm finished with all that. I'm not going back. And I'm sure as hell not dating anyone."

"But music is your life," said Smith, voice thick with emotion. "Ever since we met at the back of that truly horrible show where the bar watered down the beer and the band broke up mid-set. What a clusterfuck that was. Though we did get a drummer out of it, so it wasn't all bad."

"I mean it, Smith," said Garrett, expression set in concrete. "I'm done. I'm sick of all the bullshit. The band's finished. It's over."

"I know things went bad there for a while, but we're still your family."

A muscle ticked in the side of Garrett's jaw.

Smith sighed. "What about the house in West Hollywood? I get you selling the place in Georgia. But you're keeping the pad in L.A., right?"

"It's going up for sale."

A deep sort of sadness filled Smith's gaze. "All right. You're done with music and Los Angeles. But you've got to date someone. I promised Grace, and you know how she was about someone giving their word and not following through."

Garrett hung his head.

"It meant a lot to her . . . that you wouldn't be alone."

The only sound in the room was Joni singing "A Case of You" with heartbreaking beauty. That song I knew. And while this conversation was highly interesting, it was also *still* highly personal. I finished the second glass of wine and set the glass aside. Time to make my exit.

"You're ready for your third," said Smith, reaching out to refill my glass once more. "Good work, Ani. Nice to know that someone here has enough taste to appreciate a thirty-year-old Italian red."

"This single malt is fifty years old and probably cost more than your damn wine." Garrett raised the glass, examining the remaining contents. "I don't understand why you're saying I have no taste."

Smith just grunted.

Third glass waiting or not, I really was ready to go. Right up until I saw how miserable Smith was. The slumped shoulders and dejected expression on his handsome face. And his eyes were suspiciously liquid. This visit with his friend and former bandmate was not going well.

My ass stayed put in the chair. Even though my feet had gone numb with the weight of a sleeping dog on top of them.

"Are we really going to argue about who spent the most money on a disposable luxury item?" I asked. "Is that what we're doing?"

Smith paused. "I feel so judged."

"Right?" Garrett raised a brow. "And she accused *me* of being judgy the other day. She's just as bad."

"Hmm," said Smith, rubbing at his eyes surreptitiously.

I took a sip of wine. "That was different."

"How was it different?" asked Garrett.

"I don't know," I admitted. "This is my third glass of wine and I had a couple of beers earlier. Let me get back to you about it when I can think straight, because I am definitely right about this."

One side of his gorgeous mouth curled up, and oh wow. It was almost a smile and it was sublime. All I could do was stare.

Smith's gaze jumped between me and his friend. "Back to the dating thing."

"Man, no. I can't." Garrett curled his hands into fists. "I'm not ready."

Smith nodded. "That's understandable. If I sat around all day isolating myself from my friends and family and dwelling on my dead wife, I probably wouldn't be ready to move on either."

"Are you fucking serious right now?"

"Yeah. I am." Smith raised his chin. "If Grace could see what a miserable little sack of shit you've turned into, she'd be ashamed. And what's worse is you fucking know it."

Garrett glared at Smith and Smith glared straight back at him. Talk about tension. Apparently, Smith had finally lost his patience. When his fingers started curling into fists as well, I could stand it no longer.

"Please don't fight," I said in an almighty rush. "Physical violence makes me nauseous and this looks like a seriously expensive rug."

It might not have been pretty, but it worked. Garrett turned to me with one of his patented what-the-fuck looks. Like he couldn't quite tell if I was being serious or not. And I wasn't, but he didn't know that.

"It is," confirmed Garrett. "I don't think Gene would appreciate you vomiting on him either."

"Probably not."

"Pity." Smith downed some of his wine. "We haven't had a decent brawl in years. Could have been fun."

Garrett grunted and uncurled his fingers. Then he curled them straight back up again. "I haven't been on a date in over a decade. I wouldn't even have a fucking clue what to do."

Smith turned to look at me rather pointedly.

"What?" I asked, panicking all over again.

"I'll make some calls and talk to some people," said Garrett. "Will that do?"

Smith sighed. Again.

"I think he means for you to actually leave the safety and solitude of your woodland fortress." I bent down and scratched Gene behind the ears. It soothed me even if he slept through it. "Right?"

"I wouldn't have put it quite like that, but what she said," said Smith.

Garrett swore.

"Do I really have to go on some more about how disappointed in your life choices Grace would be?" asked Smith. "The only reason I could even get in here tonight was because you used the same damn gate code you had in L.A."

"Wait. You wouldn't have let him in?" I blurted out the question with nil thought. As you do after a night of drinking. I might not be slurring my words, but my brain was definitely not fully functional. "Are you serious?"

Our host said nothing.

As much as I hated to get loud, sometimes there was no other choice. "Garrett!"

"Of course I would have let him in," answered the man.

"You sure about that?" asked Smith.

Garrett's lips were a thin, unhappy line.

"I know your band broke up and I'm sure it's all very complicated. But isn't Smith one of your oldest friends?" My mouth would not stop. "And what about Gene? He loves you so much and he's getting on in age. Don't you want to be with him in his twilight years?"

Smith just sat back and waited. Guess I'd made his argument for him. Hooray for somewhat drunken and occasionally loud me.

For a long moment, no one said a thing. Then Garrett licked his lips. "Like you said, it's complicated."

There was a world of hurt surrounding these people. And nothing I said was helping. I finished off my third glass of wine before getting to my feet. Because it would have been rude to do otherwise. Poor Gene opened one eye and gave me a tired look. Then with a heartfelt doggy sigh, he wandered over to flop down next to Garrett's chair.

When I stood, I swayed ever so slightly. Given the lack of any strong winds, there was a small chance I was somewhat more inebriated than I'd thought. "Thank you for the wine, Smith, and it was lovely to meet you."

Garrett looked at me and frowned. Though he was always frowning. Nothing new about that. But why whatever expression on my face had bought on an even bigger and better case of the scowls on *his*, I had no idea. It's not like the man could possibly be interested in what I thought.

"Great," said Garrett. "Now you're disappointed in me too."

I cocked my head. "You care what I think?"

"You're not going to let this go, are you?" asked Garrett, turning to his friend.

"I can't," answered Smith simply.

"I know, you made her a promise." Garrett downed the remaining scotch in his glass. "What if I *don't* date someone? Would that appease you?"

Smith's brows reached for the sky. "Please explain."

"She . . ." He cleared his throat and started again. "Grace wanted me to go out and do things, right? Have a life and socialize. If I do that much, will you get off my back?"

Smith nodded.

"All right then. I'll do that with her." And he pointed at me. #wtf

Chapter Four

ARRETT SKULKED ON INTO THE GENERAL STORE THE next morning just before eight. The baseball cap was back in place, his hands shoved into his jeans pockets. Of course, drowsy and disheveled looked like high art on him. I could only pray I'd applied enough concealer to appear half human. He waited while I finished serving a red-faced teenager. The kid took her purchases and bolted just as soon as her card was approved. A couple of other local teenagers waited outside for their friend. There was much giggling going on.

"That happen often?" asked Garrett, leaning his hip against the counter.

Out front of the store, the poor kid's friends were now howling with laughter.

"What?" I asked. "You never lost a bet and had to buy a cucumber, a pack of condoms, and some lube?"

Today's frown was more contemplative than cranky. "No. Have you?"

"No, I haven't. It's pretty inventive, though, isn't it?" I

smiled, and even that hurt. My frontal lobe was seriously displeased with my recent life choices. "I am never drinking with rock stars ever again."

He almost smiled. It was a close thing.

"Coffee?"

He nodded.

Fortunately for everyone, I was able to work the machine while both half asleep and hungover. "I know why *I'm* awake. But why are *you* up this early?"

"Smith wanted to get a head start on the trip back to L.A.," he said. "He's due in the studio tonight to work with a friend."

"It still blows my mind that you two are who you are."

His gaze jumped to my face before darting away. Today's selection of cakes and pastries were enthralling, apparently.

"Is that not a cool thing to admit?"

He shrugged.

I finished making his coffee and handed it over. "It's on me. To thank you for your hospitality last night."

He gave me a sidelong glance. The dubiousness was particularly strong with him today.

"What is it, Garrett?" I asked. "You're acting even weirder than normal. Not that it isn't great that you voluntarily left your house and went somewhere."

"I wouldn't say voluntarily. And didn't you call it my woodland fortress?"

"Something like that," I agreed.

A grunt from him.

"Though 'woodland fortress' makes it sound like you have bunnies and fawns helping out around the house. Or like, acting as your bodyguards with twigs and tiny little Tasers."

He just stared at me.

"I may have slightly overdone it with the caffeine."

"Yeah," he agreed. "I wanted to talk to you about something."

"Does this have anything to do with what Smith was talking about last night?"

He tipped his chin and turned to peer around the store. Like someone might be hiding behind one of the shelves or something. Lurking, ready to jump out and ask for a selfie and an autograph. Being a celebrity must be tiring.

"There's no one else here," I said, taking a sip from my mug. Unlike his dreary drink, I fortified my caffeine with a shot of caramel. Sugar for the win.

"I've been giving it some thought."

"And you thought of someone more suitable to not date?"

"What?" His dark brows drew together tightly. "No."

"Oh."

And for a long moment, he just looked at me. Then he looked away again.

"What were you going to say, Garrett?" I asked, fingers wrapped tightly around my mug.

"There aren't really many places locally, but I promised Smith I'd try," he told the pastry case with all due seriousness. The man was the king of evading eye contact. "Do you want to come over tonight for dinner? I don't know what we'll eat. Guess I'll think of something."

"Um. Sure. That sounds nice. Sort of."

He tipped his chin.

"What time would you like me there?"

"About seven?"

"All righty then."

And he just stood there. Then he stood there some more. At long last, he said, "Give me your cell. I'll put in my number."

I grabbed my phone from under the counter and handed it over.

He paused on the screen. "Not a picture of me."

"It's a particularly cool tree I saw the other day, actually. Sorry to disappoint you."

"You're not going to give my number to anyone, are you?" he asked.

"I promise to guard your number with my life."

He didn't smile. I'd made a joke about death, for heaven's sake. How stupid. Before I could figure out how to apologize in a non-awkward fashion, he'd entered the digits and handed it back.

"Thanks," I said.

Another decisive nod and he about-faced and headed for the door with his cup of coffee in hand. The soft cotton of his T-shirt outlined his strong back and wide shoulders. Not to mention his denim-clad ass. Meanwhile, there was the whole me-having-dinner-with-a-rock-star thing to consider. And that was . . . a lot.

"Garrett," I said, voice tight. "Just a second. I have one small question. This isn't a date, right? I mean, we're not doing that, because I don't do that, and you're not ready. As previously discussed."

"Not a date," he confirmed in that smooth, deep voice with nil hesitation.

"Got it. Just friends."

"Yeah. Friends." And any weirdness or hesitation he

showed over using the F word was probably just all in my imagination. Then he was gone.

Whoa. I was officially friends with Garrett from The Dead Heart. Did not see that coming. Though I think it's safe to say that nothing about last night went the way I'd expected. Apart from winning trivia. That was pretty normal because my team was mighty.

Which was when I happened to look down and notice my red Chucks, black leggings, and oversized tee. So comfortable. But not the least bit fancy. Not even for just friends having dinner in a low-key fashion at home. Especially not when that friend was Garrett. Let's not get into why. But my fingernails were unvarnished, I wore no makeup, and my several-days-past-needing-a-wash hair was tied back in a basic boring ponytail.

It had been a while since I'd put any real concerted effort into my appearance. Four years ago, when I'd moved back to Wildwood, to be exact. When I'd decided it was easier, safer, and better to hide. If Garrett could attempt to free himself from his grief and restart his life, however, then so could I. The time had come to zhuzh me up.

Me: My truck has died outside work. It's complicated. Can we reschedule dinner?

"Oh, come on, Josh," I said, following the man around the pool table. I'd already spent a good hour following him around his auto shop. The man might be stubborn, but I was far and away worse. "You can fix it. Just one more time. For me."

"It's a dangerous rust heap and you know it," he growled. "I promised your parents last time they were in town that I wouldn't resuscitate it the next time it crapped itself and I meant it."

I threw my hands in the air. "They're lost somewhere in Canada in their Airstream. Grizzly bears have probably eaten them by now. How would they even know?"

The middle-aged man bent over the pool table, lined up his shot, and took it. "Yes," he hissed. "I am on fire tonight."

"Nice shot," said Harry, holding the other pool stick.

"What if I promise to stop teasing you about your mullet?" I asked.

Josh didn't even glance up. "I don't care what you think of my hair."

"Well, what if I promise to let your team win at trivia next week?"

At this, he paused and picked at something stuck in his teeth with his tongue. "You'd never be able to get Cézanne and Maria to agree."

I stomped a foot in frustration, because I was mature like that. And because he was right. Trivia was sacrosanct.

"You ready to go?" asked Claude, untying his apron. He'd been in the bar when I arrived, helping their cook just for fun. I have no idea why he'd ever even attempted retirement. Keeping busy was obviously his happy place. "They don't need me, after all. Not many people will be out with that storm settling in. A shame. I made some nice Angus burgers stuffed with blue cheese. But they'll keep for tomorrow."

I tried to look enthused.

Claude shook his head. "Don't tell me eating mold isn't your thing. You don't know what you're missing out on."

"It's not that I don't appreciate everything penicillin has

done for us. I just don't want it in my cheese," I said. "Thanks again for giving me a lift home."

He patted me on the arm.

The front door opened on a gust of cold wind and rain. And there stood Garrett, soaked to the bone in sneakers, jeans, and a black hoodie. Because it was coming down that damn hard outside. Everyone stopped what they were doing and stared. The fact is, dripping wet looked good on the man. Like he'd just stepped off the set of a photo shoot or a music video or something. And because he was a total stranger.

"Hey," he said, running a hand through his wet hair. He had great hair. So thick and silky. It had this wave in it that just made my fingers itch to touch. There was every chance I was a dreadful choice of not-dating friend for this man. His innate hotness hit me in the heart and groin each and every time.

"Hi there." I moved closer and lowered my voice. "What are you doing here?"

"Didn't want you stuck without a ride home in this weather."

My eyebrows were as high as the sky. "How'd you know where to find me?"

"Talked to the lady that owns the store. She was just closing up for the day."

"Ah."

"I'm driving her home," said Claude. Because of course everyone was still listening and watching.

I smiled. "It's okay. Thank you, Claude. I'll be fine with my friend here."

Claude just crossed his arms and stood there watching us.

Same as Josh and Harry. And Emma behind the bar. Awesome. We had quite the audience gathered.

"You were worried about me," I said to the rock star with no small amount of amazement.

"I texted, but you didn't answer."

"I've been busy."

"What's wrong with your car?" he asked.

"It's a heap of shit and she needs to get rid of it," said Josh, leaning on his pool stick.

"You take that back!" My mouth fell open. "Bella drove the same one in *Twilight*, only in red. That truck is iconic."

Garrett's brows went up.

"She bought it for five hundred dollars when she was seventeen and it was overdue for the junkyard then." Josh stuck out his chin. Stubborn ass of a man. "She just won't admit it."

"Four hundred," I corrected. "And it's a classic."

"How much would it cost to fix?" asked Garrett.

"It's not about money," said Josh. "The damn thing isn't safe. I don't want her getting stuck somewhere in bad weather. When was the last time it started on the first try for you?"

I frowned. "It just takes a little warming up. I bet *you* don't start on the first try anymore, either."

Claude's eyes opened painfully wide. "Ouch."

"Be reasonable, Ani." Josh sighed. "I know you love the stupid thing, but it's covered in rust and falling apart. I'd need to rebuild it from the bottom up, replace half of the engine and God knows what else. It would take time I don't have and cost you a damn fortune."

It was the empathy in his eyes that killed me. The

understanding regarding what it was like to lose a beloved vehicle. Made my stomach sink straight through the floor. "All right."

"I'll tow it to the shop and store it out back," said Josh with more of that horrible gentleness. "Give you a chance to sort out what you want to do with it."

I would not cry over a truck. How stupid. "Thank you."

With a nod, Josh went back to his game.

Garrett's hand pressed lightly against my lower back. Which was nice of him. I needed the support right about then.

"Say," said Claude, head cocked as he studied Garrett. "You look awful familiar. Don't I know you from somewhere?"

"No, he ah . . ." I stumbled for words. "He's just a friend of mine. You wouldn't know him. We should probably be going now."

And suddenly Emma screamed. "The Dead Heart! You're the lead singer of The Dead Heart! Oh my God, you're Garrett!"

Claude wrinkled his nose. "Who?"

"Huh," said Harry. "He is, too. How about that?"

Josh just frowned in confusion. He always had been more of a country music fan.

Behind the bar, Emma appeared to be in the middle of a full-on fangirl meltdown. The thirst was real. Then she said, "Remember that time we both saved his picture to the screen on our cells, Ani?"

Though I doubt Garrett even heard. His eyes were wide as the moon. With panic or fear, I don't know which. But the man was not happy. He seemed to have frozen and the situation was deteriorating rapidly. And it was kind of my fault, since he'd left the privacy of his home and come in here because he was concerned about me.

So I did the only rational thing I could and stood on a chair. "Hey. People. I have something to say."

All eyes turned to me. Including Emma's, though she continued to fan her face with her hands. Probably for the best, since she seemed a bit peaky.

The door opened, once more letting in the wind and the rain. My boss, Linda, wandered inside, patting drops of water off her face and hair. "Oh, good," she said, giving Garrett a smile. "He found you."

"Yes. Um. As I was saying . . . if a rock star had moved to Wildwood," I said, holding a finger in the air. "And I'm only saying *if*. Then it would probably be because they wanted some peace and quiet, right?"

Josh shrugged.

"Like part of the reason we all live here is because we enjoy having fewer people around and a little more space to be ourselves and so on."

"That's makes sense," Claude concurred. "It's why I moved here."

"I like the clean air and trees," said Harry.

"Sure. That too." I smiled. "But the other part of living in a small town is that we all have each other's back. And say if someone who had been through some tough times happened to move into the old Cooper house and needed a little help to blend in so they could stay, then we could do that for them, don't you think? Help them to be an accepted part of our wonderful, loving, and caring community?"

Josh smoothed back his graying mullet. "She's laying it on a bit thick."

"I want to be part of the community?" asked Garrett in a low voice. "When did I say that?"

I shushed them both.

"Lastly, I would just add one small word," I said. "Please."

No one said a damn thing.

"It was a mistake," announced Emma finally. "This man isn't Garrett from The Dead Heart."

Harry shook his head. "Well, of course he's not."

"I honestly don't care," said Josh, turning back to his game of pool.

"My mother raised me right," said Claude with all due seriousness. "Told me never to lie. But my hearing isn't what it used to be. I didn't quite catch what Emma was screaming about just before. And I can honestly say that the idea of someone famous moving to our small town has never crossed my mind. Seems to me, you're just a new neighbor looking to slow down a little like the rest of us. No rock stars here. Just . . ." Claude tapped his chin. "Gary."

Garrett's brows rose. "Gary?"

"Yes," said Claude.

"You don't want to pick a pseudonym that's maybe a little bit further removed from his actual name?" I suggested.

"I had an Uncle Gary. It's a fine name and it's already decided," said Claude. And that was that.

"Quite a stirring speech, Ani." Linda smiled at us both. "Nice to properly meet you, dear. Your secret's safe with us."

"Thank you, ma'am."

"You know, I feel such a connection to you. Almost as if

we're family." Without another word, Linda wandered off to get a drink.

Garrett shook his head and extended his hand to me. "Get down before you fall down."

I slipped my hand into his and gave him my most beauteous grin. "Welcome to Wildwood, Gary."

"You had a picture of me on your cell." The handsome idiot took a big bite of his Angus beef and blue cheese burger.

I popped another onion ring into my mouth. It was a large one, but I was determined. Mostly, I was determined to not speak. But filling the belly with comfort food is also a noble cause.

"Not going to say anything?" he asked.

I waited till I'd finished chewing. "I choose not to dignify it with a response."

We were huddled in a booth at the back of the bar. Safe from any prying eyes. Mostly. Not that many more people had come into the bar. Emma and Harry were taking Garrett's situation seriously. Any newcomers were fed the cover story. And anyone who looked over once too often was subjected to a long and confusing conversation from Linda. I think she was claiming Gary as some long-lost nephew. That she had neither siblings nor any other family connections to possibly provide her with same would be kept on the down low.

Claude had been keen on feeding Garrett one of his burgers. And despite being damp, Garrett had agreed to stay. Maybe he was readier to return to life than he wanted to admit. Maybe he was lonely. Maybe he was just hungry. Whatever the cause, our not-date was going ahead. Conversation was being made with great care. On my part at least.

I took a sip of water. "Though I will say it's ungentlemanly of you to keep bringing up something that happened on Margarita Night."

"They have a Margarita Night?"

"Last Friday of the month," I confirmed. "Things have a habit of happening."

"Things that should never be discussed again?"

"Exactly."

A small, amused smile curled his lips, making my heart stutter. The man was a health hazard. "What does that look mean?" he asked.

I gazed at him, thought it over, and ate another onion ring. In that order. "Since you're already teasing me about this alleged photo . . ."

"Hmm?"

"Wouldn't the first rule of not-dating club have to be 'don't be attracted to your not-date'?"

"Actually," he said, "it would be 'don't talk about not-dating club.'"

"To the media, et cetera."

"That's right." He downed some of his beer. "I don't see how the photo is a problem, in all honesty. You liked the idea of me. How I looked on a particular day when someone had fucked around with my hair and chosen my clothes for me, most likely. That's not me. It's a commodity packaged for sale."

I said a whole lot of nothing.

He shrugged and took another bite of the burger, juice from

the creation running down his chin. With a careless hand, he wiped it away with a napkin. "What?"

"I was bedazzled by the glamor and lights, huh?"

"Basically."

"So I'm not actually really attracted to you. Okay," I said with some relief. "Let's roll with that."

The little line appeared between his brows and the furrowed forehead was back. "On the other hand, maybe I don't mind if you *are* attracted to me. It's just not that big a deal."

"Is that so?" I narrowed my eyes on him. "This is fascinating. Let me guess: you're so used to people being attracted to you that it doesn't even really register with you anymore."

He gave another of those shrugs. So much nonchalance.

"Hubris is the word of the day."

"The music industry is every bit as driven by looks as it is talent. More so, even. It sucks, but it's true." A hint of a smile appeared again. "It's why I'm lead singer and not Smith."

I snorted. "Oh, yeah. Because he so clearly fell out of the ugly tree and hit every branch on the way down."

The furrows in his forehead made another appearance.

"What? Am I not allowed to look at your friend in an appreciative manner?"

"Do what you like," he mumbled, and set to finishing the last of his food with much relish.

"How's your burger?"

"It's great," he said, sounding more than a little surprised.

"Claude knows his stuff." I smiled. "You'll be able to tell Smith that you ate out and socialized."

"Should get him off my back for a bit." He carefully wiped

his hands. "The other thing about being attracted to someone is, for it to mean anything deeper, you have to actually know them."

"And I don't know you?"

A hint of a smirk curled the edge of his lips. "Not because I'm complicated or anything. Just ... we only met. You know my music and you've seen my picture. But it's not the same thing."

"Okay."

He raised a brow. "You agree with me?"

"Yes."

"Amazing," he said. "You know, I've probably talked more with you tonight than I've talked in years."

"How does it feel?"

He paused and pondered. "Okay, actually."

"Good. I'm glad. I like this for you. This whole bravely-going-forth-and-interacting-with-the-world thing."

"Do you sleep with the lights on?" he asked out of nowhere. "It's just, I'm usually up most of the night and sleep during the day."

"Like a vampire."

"Like a musician," he corrected. "I happened to notice the lights over at your place are often on till early in the morning."

I fiddled with the placement of my glass of water and the assorted condiments. As you do. "Leaving aside the part where you've been watching me again, the truth is ... I don't always sleep so great."

"Why is that?"

I shrugged.

He frowned.

"Busy brain. I don't know. It's not a big deal," I said, rushing right along. "Let's talk about you. You've traveled the world and experienced all sorts of things. Much more interesting than me and my wonky sleep habits and various neuroses."

"I don't know about that."

With all due caution, he turned his head to the side and checked out the place. He sat slouched back in the booth, at ease. There didn't appear to be an iota of tension in him. Not how I'd been expecting the man to react to a public place. Perhaps he was just that happy not to be in L.A.

As for the rest of the room, Harry and Linda were seated at the bar drinking and chatting with Emma, with a couple of locals playing pool and a few more eating. Otherwise, all was quiet, give or take the music coming from the jukebox. Garrett's fingers tapped out an intricate beat against the scarred wooden tabletop.

"Do you miss making music?" I asked. "I know you talked about it a bit last night. But—"

"No." He took a deep breath and let it out slowly. Then he narrowed his eyes on me all contemplative like. "You know what? Second rule of not-dating: no personal questions."

"We're going to wind up talking about the weather at this rate."

"Probably," he conceded.

"How is Gene doing? Can I ask that?"

"He's settling in fine. He, ah . . . it's good having him around again. For both of us." Once more, he looked over his shoulder around the bar. It seemed any concession made regarding the giving of information was accompanied by the temporary removal of eye contact. Like things had gotten too personal and he needed a minute to recoup. The man was amazingly adept at hiding in plain sight. "This place isn't bad."

"It has a certain rustic charm."

"That was kind of them to go along with keeping quiet about me."

"Yeah. It was. They're good people," I said. "I know Wildwood is small, but it has a lot to offer."

"What do you do with your free time?" he asked. "Go hiking?"

"Hell no." I snorted. "I don't do nature up close. A nice big window or patio with a drink in hand is sufficient for me. Just sit back, relax, and enjoy the view, you know?"

"Remind me why you live here again."

"Well, I grew up here," I said. "It's what I know. And the area is beautiful and the people are quite often great. But you specified no personal questions. That means I get to ask you one."

His gaze turned unhappy. "We're trading answers now?"

"It's only fair."

His mouth firmed and for a long moment, he just stared at me. Like he was preparing himself to take a hit or something. For life to hurt him once again. It was sad to see.

"You already answered my question about Gene, so . . ." I said quietly.

Neither of us spoke for a minute.

"The sky was a pretty shade of blue today," I commented, apropos of nothing.

"This is you talking about the weather?"

I just shrugged.

"Go on," he growled. "Ask your question."

"Thank you." I smiled. "Why don't you have any tattoos?"

He paused, surprised. "Not a big fan of needles."

"Ah."

"That's it? That's your question?"

"Yep."

He pondered this for a moment. And I think he was pleased, but it was hard to tell. "So what can we do on our next not-date?"

"You want to go out with me again?"

"As friends. Sure. This hasn't been so bad."

"I agree." I nodded. "And as friends only. In which case, it would probably be more accurate to describe these events as simply outings instead of not-dates, right?"

"The word *date* upsets you that much?"

I gave him my best fake smile. "Of course not. It's just . . ."

"What?"

"Nothing. Call it what you want. Your choice of word does not affect me at all."

"Okay. Let me get back to you with a time and place. I do have one more vaguely personal question, though," he said, face a perfect blank. "Did you have a photo of Smith on your cell?"

I gave him a slow smile. "I'll never tell."

Chapter Five

"Let me see if I got this right," said Cézanne, sitting in the driver's seat of the secondhand vehicle we'd taken for a test drive. After hitting up the farmers' market in Falls Creek, of course. "A famous rock star moved in next door to you and you didn't tell anybody."

"Yes."

"I'm not sure if I should be impressed at your ability to keep your mouth shut or upset at your inability to trust your friends to also keep *their* mouths shut." She shook her head. Then she patted the Jeep Wrangler's dashboard. Due to growing up helping her father, who was a professional at restoring cars, she knew all about motors. "This is a good compact SUV that runs well, hasn't done too many miles for its age, and is in the right price range. If you don't buy it, I probably will. We could use a backup vehicle."

"I'll take it," I said. "Josh found a buyer for my truck who wants to use it for parts. He got me an okay price, actually."

"Good."

"I'm sorry I didn't tell you," I said. "I just . . . I don't know. Something about his sad, moody ass got to me. Or maybe it was that he expected me to blab to everyone within a twenty-mile radius."

"You do enjoy being contrary."

"I really do. Forgive me?"

"Of course. The truth is, we're adults. We can mind our own business and keep our own secrets now and then." She smiled. "So you're hoping the whole town will fall for this Gary thing? That should be interesting."

"Eh. I think some people will just respect his privacy on principle. As for the others, it's not like you expect to see a rock star in Wildwood," I said. "And Linda has been working overtime with her nephew story."

Cézanne made a humming noise. "I bet she's enjoying herself immensely."

"If I have to listen to how it reminds her of the time she met Hendrix at Woodstock one more time, it's entirely possible I'll scream. Or just continue to suffer in silence with a really pained expression."

"I think Garrett will be okay," she said. "Wildwood looks after their own. No wonder you decided to protect him if he moved here and tried to hide out from civilization while generally being in a bad mood. Reminds me of when *you* moved back to town."

And the less said about the topic, the better. I opened the passenger-side door, ready to go haggle over price. "Wish me luck."

By the time we settled on the vehicle and got back to town, Maria was waiting at my place. Cézanne's husband was busy practicing with his garage band and Maria's girlfriend was away on a work trip, so we were spending Saturday night together.

"Shiny silver," said Maria, checking out my new wheels. "You happy with it?"

"Yeah." I smiled. "I'll miss the truck, but . . ."

Cézanne pulled up in her Tahoe behind me. "We found her some wheels."

"Thank you again," I said.

"You're welcome." She smiled. "Now feed me."

"What movie are we watching?" asked Maria.

"It's your turn to choose," I reminded her.

In comparison to the grand old Victorian next door, my home was modest. A log cabin built an eon ago, with a stone fireplace and wooden walls, floors, and cabinets. Very atmospheric if you were after that I'm-just-here-to-commune-with-nature-and-kill-animals kind of vibe. It was, however, mine all mine. One day I'd have the money to renovate, put in a new kitchen. No time soon, given my savings had just gone toward a vehicle.

But oh well. I liked my space. I'd filled it with some vintage pieces found in antique stores and garage sales. A battered kitchen table with cool mismatched chairs. An old navy-blue wooden toy box for storing firewood. And a red sofa and a large wicker chair loaded with cushions and throws for lounging upon. The mix of colors reminded me on the bad nights, when I couldn't sleep and couldn't settle, that this was my home and everything was okay. That my fear was just a bad habit.

We wound up eating chicken salad in front of *28 Days Later*. Despite choosing the movie, Maria spent most of the time hanging over by the window.

"All I'm saying is, if zombies can run, we're screwed." I

speared some chicken and spinach with my fork. "No one would be left."

"Imagine being one of the last people left alive with Cillian Murphy, though."

"I'm not saying no."

"What did you put in this Green Goddess dressing?" asked Cézanne. "Something's different."

"Since you don't eat anchovies, I thought I'd try capers." She nodded. "Nice."

"Claude suggested it."

"I see him. He's out with his dog." Maria waved her hand. "Hello, Mr. Rock Star. Good day to you and your particularly large pet."

"I'm basically just waiting for him to plant a hedge between our houses," I said. "Or an even bigger fence without the fancy iron sections that people can see through. Top it off with a little barbed wire, perhaps."

Cézanne nodded. "Probably be for the best."

"He saw me. Oh! He's raising his hand in greeting," reported Maria. "No smile, though."

"Smiling isn't really his thing," I said.

"I'm beginning to see why you didn't tell us." Cézanne shook her head. "Woman, sit down, would you?"

With a grin, Maria deposited herself on the wicker chair. "At least I can say I've seen a celebrity in the flesh now."

My cell chimed.

Garrett: Visitors?

Me: A highly curious friend. She's calming down now. My apologies.

"Ruh-roh," I said. "You got me into trouble with him."

Maria winced. "Sorry. Tell him I really like his band. The early stuff, mostly. The move away from acoustic into more of a hard rock sensibility kind of lost me, in all honesty."

"I will definitely get right on that."

"Wouldn't it be great if you two got together?" asked Maria, all enthused.

I snorted. "Romance? In this economy?"

Maria laughed.

"What's going on with you?" asked Cézanne. "You're very excitable today. Not that it's a bad thing."

"I have news," confessed Maria, sitting up straight. "I applied for a job in San Francisco. And I just heard back this morning—I got it!"

"You're leaving?" I asked with a frown.

"That's great." Cézanne clapped her hands. "Congratulations!"

Maria beamed.

I gave her my best fake smile. "Wow. That's wonderful."

"I know I was resistant to the idea of her dating. But now that Mama's got Claude, I don't have to worry about her being on her own so much. It freed us up to make the move. It's a promotion for me and a pathway to better money for Danielle," she said. "And we'll be close to her family for a change, which will be nice."

Cézanne smiled. "We'll sure miss you on trivia nights."

"I'm only a phone call away if you don't know the answer to a question. Which is totally against the rules." Maria laughed. "Can you imagine? Heather would lose her mind."

"We're really going to miss you," I said. "But if it's what you and Danielle want, then I'm happy for you."

"Thanks. I'm going to miss you guys too."

Security checks were an important part of my nighttime routine. Given the size of the cabin, it was impressive how long I could drag out the ritual.

I started at the tiny window in the bathroom that no one could even fit through before moving on to the larger ones in my bedroom. I'd installed key-operated locks to complement the latches. Next came the window on the side of the main room that looked out onto my neighbor's property, and the ones with a view onto the front porch. Then came the front and back doors with their various deadbolts and safety chains, and so on. Often I'd repeat this process two or three times. Just to be sure.

The only light outside was the one glowing in the distance—Garrett's parlor. I wasn't the lone person in town awake at one in the morning. And I had to be up in five hours. No wonder the dark smudges under my eyes were so damn big. I'd already done a sheet facial and some random reading on Wikipedia to increase my trivia knowledge. Then I'd started *The Girl with Stars in Her Eyes* by Xio Axelrod. Anytime was a good time to read a romance. And rock stars were a current area of interest for me.

Which was when a shadow filled the parlor window in the house next door.

Damn. I'd been busted. But then again, so had he.

Garrett: Lurking?

Me: More like skulking.

Garrett: Can't sleep?

Me: No.

The little dots bounced on screen to show he was typing something. But nothing appeared. Then the shadow moved away from the window. So as not to look like a psychopath, I headed back into my bedroom, turning off lights as I went. My body and brain were weary and my bones ached, I was so damn tired. Yet that same stupid wired tension ran through me. Sleep had to happen sooner or later. Surely.

In the darkness, the cabin was quiet, the night still. Not that it helped. Being alone was both a choice and a chore. But the knowledge that he was right there next door was actually kind of nice. To not feel so isolated out here on the edge of town. My cell buzzed on the bedside table.

Garrett: I'll be up for a while if you want to talk.

Me: Thanks.

Me: Was your day ok?

Garrett: Yeah. Yours?

Me: Good.

Garrett: You seeing someone about your sleep?

Garrett: Shit. I said no personal questions. Forget it.

Me: It's fine. Going to try lying down again. Night.

It was a little alarming how life started to revolve around

the rock star. Not because I couldn't stop thinking about him (though he did have a tendency to live in my head rent free), but due to the residents of Wildwood becoming increasingly obsessed. Which was how I came to be knocking on his door Friday afternoon. Six days after our early-morning texting and a whole week and a half after our impromptu meal at the bar. During which time there'd been no mention of the second not-date. I may or may not have been ghosted by Garrett. Whatever. He was free to do as he pleased and I had my own life to live.

I definitely didn't dress up or put on makeup for the man. My white tee, blue jeans, and violet-colored Chucks would do just fine for this visit.

"Ani," he said with his usual frown in place. "Smith gave you the code to the gate."

I sighed and set down the two large bags and one sizeable box. "Yes. I'm sorry to intrude. But you haven't been answering your cell or responding to recent texts."

The frown amped up to a scowl. Such heavy dark brows and stormy blue eyes.

"Which I agree is your right, so stop scowling at me. However, Smith is worried, and some of these items are time sensitive."

"What is all this?"

"Mostly more food. They didn't want to leave it at your gate and risk having it eaten by animals or you not seeing it was there," I explained. "Linda made you chocolate chip cookies. I'm pretty sure there's cannabis in them, so beware. And Emma from the bar crocheted you a lovely blanket that should match the colors in your parlor. She was worried about how you were going to handle your first winter up here even though

67

it's a while away yet. There's also some cornbread and chili that Claude dropped off today and other assorted goods. I got them to attach a note or at least their name so you know who made what if you'd like to say thanks."

"There's a lot."

"Well, they're excited that you're here and they want to make you feel welcome," I said. "And no one has narced you out that I'm aware of. The Gary story didn't work as well as we hoped. I may have been overestimating certain people's gullibility. But Linda put the fear of God and the threat of reporters and your fans inundating the town into those who might have talked. While we could probably do with the money, no one wants mayhem on Main Street. So I think you're safe for now."

Some of the tension in his rigid shoulders seemed to ease.

"And Smith said if you don't call him back he's coming back up here." I pasted on a smile. "That's everything. I'm going to go now. Bye."

"Wait. I, ah . . ."

Gene stuck his doggy nose through the gap between Garrett and the door. Much panting ensued as he wriggled and worked his way out to me.

I commenced giving him pats. "How are you, beautiful boy?"

"I didn't get back to you about our . . . you know," he said. "Our second not-date. Sorry."

"It's fine."

He looked at me and I looked at him, and ugh. He was just too much. The hint of unhappy in his gaze matched the stern lines of his face. "Are you just saying that or is it fine?"

I opened my mouth and then shut it again.

"Right," he said, and let out a breath. "How have you been?"

"Um. Good. And you?"

"Good. Yeah." He shoved a hand through his messy hair. A crumpled black tee, black jeans, and no shoes. There were small dark hairs on his toes. Not excessive. But they were there. And why I was once again staring at his feet was anyone's guess. "About what I texted the other night. I didn't mean to—"

"I don't mind you asking me personal questions, Garrett. Though as just displayed, I may not always know how to answer them at the time."

He just stared at me.

"It only seems fair that you can ask me questions, given I can get the basics about your life off Wikipedia and TMZ," I said. "But like you said, I don't really know you. We've only talked in person like, what, four times?"

"Five," he corrected.

"Five. Right."

"Not including now." He crossed his arms and leaned against the doorjamb. "You were saying?"

"It's just that the not-sleeping issue isn't something I tend to talk about, and I'm reluctant to dump my years-old trauma on you without fair warning," I finished in a rush. "And now that I've raised things to a whole new level of awkward, I'm definitely going to go."

"It was her birthday the other day."

"Oh."

"That's why I went quiet, and why Smith is probably blowing up your phone."

I just nodded.

"Do you want to come in?" he asked, his gaze on the

packages at his feet. Guess we both had avoidance issues. "It's a mess, but . . ."

"Are you asking just to be polite?"

He cleared his throat and narrowed his eyes on me. "Ani, I don't know if you've noticed, but I don't really tend to do things just to be polite."

"In that case, I'd like to come in."

He wasn't lying about it being a mess. Glasses and mugs and plates sat abandoned on the coffee table in the parlor. Records, an acoustic guitar, and scraps of paper lay scattered around. The fading sunlight seemed to fill the old Cooper house with shadows and memories.

We hauled his collection of goodies into the kitchen. It had cool vintage-mosaic-style blue and white tiles on the floor, dark blue cabinets, a stainless-steel farmhouse sink, and a white stone countertop. A similar sleek but vintage aesthetic to the parlor. And there were a whole lot more dirty plates, glasses, and silverware, along with an empty bottle of scotch or two.

"Shit," he muttered as he cleared some space at the long wooden table. "Sit. Please."

I did as asked, and Gene promptly settled down for a nap atop of my feet.

"I'm just going to . . ." And he started gathering up all of the dirty dishes and loading the dishwasher. Like he was actually embarrassed at me seeing the state of his place. I was going to ask if I could help, but watching him work was kind of nice.

Then, out of nowhere, he ordered, "Tell me something personal."

"What?"

"Anything. I don't care."

"Why?"

The man actually seemed flustered. "Because, as you might have guessed, I'm a little fucked up about trusting people. And I feel like we're still trading personal information, and I want to tell you something. But it's your turn to give, so . . ."

"Um. Okay," I said, and took a deep breath. "My favorite teacher was my third-grade teacher, Miss Reyne. She was cool. We read a lot of books and did interesting art projects."

"That's not very personal."

"You said anything."

"Yeah." He finished filling the top tray of the dishwasher. "But you can do better than that."

"How about, I tell people my favorite book is *Pride and Prejudice* by Jane Austen, but it's actually this one that involves monster fucking called *Ice Planet Barbarians*."

"That *is* interesting, but no. Try again."

"God. I don't know." I shrugged. "I'm wearing violet-colored underwear. Will that do? Is that personal enough for you?"

His brows rose. "You pick your underwear to match your Chucks?"

"Shit." Damn me and my mouth. Because of course he had to go and make the connection between my sneaker and panties. "Maybe. Sometimes. Fine. All of the time. It's like a good luck thing. I've been doing it for so long I feel weird if the color of my shoes and panties don't match. Let's stop talking about it now."

He considered this information for a moment. "Okay."

"So glad I passed the test," I mumbled, my face as hot as a forge.

"I feel guilty about you."

"You . . . what? You feel *guilty* about me?"

"Yeah," he said, and continued packing the plates. "I know we're not doing anything. Just being friends, but I feel guilty about you, and that's the first time that's happened."

"All right."

"This information doesn't require anything of you," he said. "I mean, the fact that you only want to be friends kind of makes you safe. But I've been doing some thinking, and you and I are getting to know each other and I'm attempting to show some trust. If I disappear or go silent or whatever, just give me time, yeah?"

I nodded.

"I'll be honest with you: my life would be simpler if we didn't hang out." He glanced at me out of the corner of his eye as he kept on being busy. "But as Smith rightly pointed out, the last few years have been shit and not much of a life at all. Isolating myself . . . it's not good. She, ah . . . Grace would have called bullshit on me a long time ago. That's the truth."

I nodded again.

"Say something."

"Ah. I hear you. I find feelings regarding pretty much any- thing to be deeply confusing, so I understand that time and space are often required to process them."

"Yeah," he agreed, leaning his hip against the kitchen counter. And the sudden speculative gleam in his gaze was not comforting. "Can't believe you told me the color of your panties. That really came out of nowhere. Do you normally tell people that?"

"No. No, I do not. Nor will I ever again, rest assured."

"Interesting," he said, sounding way too fucking amused. "Are you hungry? Want some chili and cornbread?"

"Yes, please."

"Matching shoes and panties," he muttered, moving around the kitchen. And strangely enough, he almost sounded kind of happy.

But I still said, "Shut up, please, Garrett."

Chapter Six

MORNINGS WERE SLOW ONCE THE EARLY-MORNING COFFEE rush was finished. Seeing Garrett standing in the general store doorway dressed in a loose muscle shirt, cut-off sweatpants, and sneakers on a Tuesday was surprising, to say the least. With a sheen of sweat glistening on his tanned skin in the morning light, it became obvious to me that this whole friend thing might be trickier than I'd first thought. My hormones were all but rioting at the sight of him. I had adapted to his general hotness being all up in my face. But this . . . holy shit.

Though, he had been made aware of my fangirl status and said he didn't care. Now if I could just ignore the rush of dopamine he inspired.

"You left your woodland fortress." I stepped back from my chalk-art masterpiece. It was time to update the coffee shop menu. "To what do we owe the honor?"

He blew out a breath and gave me his patented *I am vaguely amused by you* gaze. "When you fell over 'cause you were laughing so hard at me living here and using a treadmill, I thought it might be time to get out and try some of the tracks around town."

"To be fair, I had eaten two of Linda's cookies."

He grunted.

"And you never leaving the house was ridiculous."

"Those cookies will get you," said Claude, seated at one of the small, round café tables with an espresso. "What track did you take?"

Garrett grabbed a glass and helped himself to the free filtered water at the end of the counter. He chugged down two glasses. "Along the river."

"Nice."

"A few people out fishing."

"Always. This time of year they'll be after the salmon. But there's swimming or even rafting farther downstream if fishing isn't your thing." Claude got to his feet. "I better get a move on. Lupita wants to head to Falls Creek for lunch and to do some shopping."

"Have a nice time," I said, putting the selection of chalk markers in my apron pocket.

Garrett and Claude exchanged nods. Then the rock star came over to check out the menu. The swooping script I'd chosen for the heading and the more rigid sans serif I'd used for the item descriptions. He even leaned in close to check out the detail on the drawings of coffee beans and so on. "You're good at this."

"Thanks. Visual merchandising is sort of my thing."

"Is that what you studied?"

"Yeah," I said. "You want coffee?"

"No, I was just stopping by to say hi."

"You're allowed to do that. If I'd known mocking you would

have gotten you out of that house, I'd have tried sooner. What do you even do in there all on your own?"

"I'm not on my own, there's Gene. And I've actually been working the last week or so," he said. "I've started writing again."

"Garrett, that's great."

"Yeah." He turned away. "Lot of empty shops on Main Street."

"Ugh. A whole bunch of buildings were owned by a local man. But when he died they went to his nephew, who lives in Texas and has no understanding of the local economy. The idiot tripled the rent and forced just about everyone out of business. We get some tourists up here, but not enough to support that kind of sudden increase," I explained. "Didn't I already complain to you about this? I think I did."

"Thought you didn't want more people inundating the place."

"I don't want you to have to go into hiding because of paparazzi or a pack of your fans descending on the town. But a certain amount of growth leading to more money coming into the community would be a good thing," I said. "There has to be a happy medium between more exposure for the town and total chaos. Then we could fund the repairs that the town hall and library need, for a start."

"What about the old theater?"

"That place has been closed for forever. It's pretty much only used by ghost hunters and teens looking for a place to hang out."

"Is that what you used to do?"

"Oh yeah." I smiled. "We'd drink booze someone had stolen from their parents, talk smack about everything and anything, and dream about the day we got out of this place."

"And yet here you are."

"That's the funny thing about life," I said. "How you feel about things can change dramatically. Let's talk about something else. Like the fact that this Friday is Margarita Night."

He cocked his head. "You don't say."

"I do say. Are you coming?"

"You make it sound like a dare."

"Maybe it is."

For a moment, he stood there in silence. Then his jaw firmed and he said, "Sure. Why not?"

"Good for you."

"It can be our next not-date."

"Um, yeah. Okay."

The side of his lips twitched. Then his gaze dropped to the floor and hit upon my shoes. A pair of green Chucks, to be precise. And the silence was loaded as fuck.

I groaned.

"What color, exactly, would you call that?"

"Sage green," I said. "But is that really something you should be asking a person who's just a friend?"

His gaze jumped to my face and he said a whole lot more of nothing. Such a great blank expression. I had no idea what he was thinking. Then he muttered, "Good question."

"Time to change the subject again. Fun fact," I said. "When you see me hanging out at windows late at night it's because I'm checking the locks. I have this ritual that involves going over all of the security in my cabin at least a few times. It helps me relax and go to sleep. At least, it does in theory. And that's not normally something I discuss with other people, just so you know."

"All right," he said cautiously.

I smiled to show him all was well.

"But, Ani, I'm not worried about you spying on me. Not really."

"I wasn't spying on you. I don't spy on you." I raised my voice ever so slightly. "That's part of the point I was making."

"What was the other part?"

"That involved me giving you a piece of personal information. Thereby making it your turn again so that you can tell me something if or when you feel like it."

He blinked. "Okay. Thanks."

"You're welcome." I moved around to the other side of the counter as Josh wandered in from the gas station. He yawned so hard his jaw cracked, and my brows rose in surprise. "One shot or two, my friend?"

Josh held up three fingers.

"Ouch."

"We minded the baby for Emma last night," he explained. "I'd forgotten how loud they can be. Babies might look all little and cute, but I'm telling you, they are pure evil when they won't sleep."

I made him his coffee and handed it over. "I believe you."

Josh sipped his beverage, fluffed up the back of his mullet, and left the building without further ado.

As I charged the coffee to Josh's account, Garrett stared after the man with interest.

"What?" I asked.

"He honestly doesn't give a shit that I'm here."

"Country music fan," I said. "A very tired one, apparently. But if you were Dolly Parton or Willie Nelson, rest assured, he would lose his ever-loving mind. Is indifference really so rare?"

"I don't know. Guess it's just been a while since I haven't had to try and hide who I am. I had a beard in France and New Zealand. That helped. But now . . ."

"You're out in the open. How does it feel?"

He paused. "Good."

"I'm glad. It's not always easy coming out of hiding."

"No, it isn't."

Which was when Magda, the local hairstylist, entered the store and stopped stone-cold dead with her mouth hanging open and her cell clutched to her chest. She was an older white woman with a cool gray pixie cut. "Garrett. Oh my. It really is you."

He nodded. "Ma'am."

"I want you to know," she whisper-hissed as she got good and close, "your secret is safe with us and you are very welcome in our town."

"Thank you."

"And I am so sorry for your loss. My partner Teddy passed a little while back and . . . it's not easy. There are still days now and then when it all seems like a bad dream."

"Yeah," he agreed.

"You take care of yourself, honey."

"Thank you, ma'am. Excuse me." A deep line had appeared between his brows. Then he gave us both another nod and was gone.

"Not much of a talker, is he?" said Magda, inspecting the pastry cabinet.

"He can be shy. I thought he did quite well."

"Maybe he'll have more words for me next time." She flashed me a smile. "I'll have one of Claude's almond croissants."

"You got it. By the way," I said, grabbing a brown paper bag, "you know how you've been carefully hinting for a while now that you'd like to do my hair?"

"I believe what I've been openly saying for the past few years is that it's time for you to stop cutting your own hair in the kitchen like a toddler and let me style that straggly mess for you."

"That's a little harsh, but I'll allow it."

"Holy shit," she gasped. "Has my lucky day finally come? Are you at long last ready to bid adieu to those damn split ends?"

I smiled. "You know what, Magda? I think I am."

Change can be scary. There's comfort in the known. It requires nothing new of you. And who's to say how others will react? In a small town where everyone knows everything, change is especially terrifying. Because, like it or not, people are going to tell you their opinions and then some.

"Did I really look that bad before?" I took a sip of my prickly pear margarita. "I mean, really?"

"Of course not," said Cézanne. "Ignore them."

From the time I stepped foot in the bar to when my ass met the black vinyl seat in our usual booth in the corner, I received no less than eleven comments and three gasps of surprise. Talk about excessive. Maybe I should have been wearing a paper bag over my head for the last four years. Their reactions seemed to suggest as much.

A humorous golden banner proclaiming good riddance hung above the jukebox, and Maria and Danielle were holding court by the bar. Everyone wanted to buy them a drink. And everyone had words of advice for them regarding dealing with the outside world. How best to hold onto your soul in the big city. They would be sorely missed in Wildwood.

"Are you free tomorrow?" asked Cézanne. "We got a late booking of a busload of tourists wanting to do a tasting and I'm low on staff with that flu going around."

"Sure. What time do you need me there?"

"Just before eleven would be great. Thank you."

"Hey." Garrett appeared at the end of the booth. And stopped and stared. Like seriously, the man gaped at me.

My shoulders slumped. "Not you too."

"We haven't met properly, have we? Hello, Garrett. I'm Cézanne." She got to her feet. "If you'll excuse me, it is time for me to go beat my husband at pool. You can take my seat, since I don't need to be present for the words you two are about to exchange."

"Nice to meet you," he said, before turning back to me. Then he licked his lips and sat down. "Busy in here tonight."

I stirred my drink with the paper straw. "Get a haircut and put on a little makeup and the whole damn town loses their mind. And this is not some attempt to get into your pants, so take that look off your face. Holy shit."

He opened his mouth and then audibly snapped it shut. Wise man.

"Just because I'm not wearing a tee." I plucked at the shoe-string strap on my navy linen top. "I like to be comfortable and I hate ironing. But wanting to be pretty occasionally for myself isn't a crime."

"Okay," said Garrett eventually. Then he picked up my drink and downed a mouthful. "I needed that."

"Well hey there, Ani," said the minister from the local church. "Don't you look all dressed up and pretty for a change?"

I gave him my best fake smile. "Thank you, Mr. Gardner."

"Are we going to see you on Sunday?"

"No, Mr. Gardner. I hear it's just fine in Hell this time of year. Guess I'll take my chances."

He waggled a finger at me like I was a naughty child and headed for his table.

"Jerk." I scoffed. "Give me strength. They all think this is about you, but it's really not. It was just time."

Garrett rested his hands on the table with his fingers meshed. "You decided to stop hiding too."

"Yeah." I rested back against the bench. "It didn't seem right to lecture you without doing some work on myself."

"I can see that."

"You know, I used to dress up sometimes when I was younger. They've forgotten. I used to wear lipstick and mascara and the occasional low-cut blouse with my jeans. It never used to cause this much of a fuss."

"You're allowed to dress how you like."

"Yes, I am." I finished off my drink. "I could just do without all of the attention."

He gazed around the room. "They're not looking at you anymore, they're looking at me."

I snorted. Then I checked. "So they are. Good work."

"Apart from the guy over at the second pool table." He scowled. "He needs to put his fucking eyes back inside his head."

"That's Christian. We went to school together. He was actually my first kiss when I was twelve," I said. "By the end of school that day, he'd already dumped me for another. That's when I learned that love doesn't last."

Garrett's scowl did not improve.

Then he turned his head and took me in. From the carefully constructed messy bun on top of my head to my dark eyeliner, long lashes, and glossy lips. While I'd always had concealer around to deal with the scar on my neck, this was a whole new level of makeup artistry on display. I may or may not have had to watch several videos to remind me how to do it all right. His gaze lowered to the neckline of my camisole for a brief moment before returning to my face.

"Well?" I asked.

"You dressed up for yourself. Not because of me."

"That's right."

He scratched at his stubble. "If I comment on how you look are you going to tear me a new one?"

"No. You're permitted. I asked for your opinion."

"Here we go." Emma slid a couple more margaritas and an array of soft tacos, with guacamole and street corn, onto the table. "Hi, Garrett. Nice to see you again."

He gave her the chin tip. "Emma."

"Oh," she said dreamily. "He knows my name."

Once Emma left, I said, "I ordered for us. The kitchen tends to get busy on nights like this."

"Thanks," he said. "Looks good."

"Wait until you taste it. Maria's mom, Lupita, and Claude have taken over the kitchen tonight. It's Maria and Danielle's last night in town. They're moving to San Francisco for work."

"You mentioned something about that the other day."

"Yeah. We spent last weekend packing up their place," I said.

"I'll introduce you once the crowd around them calms down a little."

He nodded.

"You never gave me your verdict on my appearance."

"Hey, now." He raised his brows. "What is this? Are you fishing for compliments?"

"Shut up, Garrett," I grumbled. "Like I even care about your opinion."

The hint of a smile made another appearance as he gazed around the room again. But it soon disappeared. A familiar guitar riff filled the room and the sound of Grace's voice poured out of the jukebox. It was soon accompanied by Garrett singing about being high on love.

Lots of eyes turned our way and several people cheered. Of all the songs for someone to choose to play.

Oh, shit.

"It's fine," he told the tabletop.

While it wasn't my business to tell him how to manage his grief, avoiding his dead wife wasn't going to work. Obviously. Smith had dabbled in exposure therapy when he'd visited and it had seemed to help Garrett.

"Your voices really complemented each other," I said, softly. "Haven't heard this one in a while."

He grunted. Then he shoved a taco in his mouth.

"You didn't do many songs together, did you?"

He swallowed and washed it down with water. "No. Not many."

I kept on playing with the straw in my drink.

"Grace was a perfectionist." He picked up a napkin and wiped his mouth. "We drove each other fucking crazy in the recording studio. She'd do take after take after take. Be there till four in the morning. Don't get me wrong, I like to get things right. But she just didn't know when to stop. It was better if we didn't work together outside of touring and writing together now and then. But yeah . . . we recorded a couple of songs."

"How did you meet?" I asked.

"She was doing a festival with a friend. Went backstage to say hello and there she was. Took her a while to agree to give me a chance. She'd sworn off dating people in the industry. Can't really blame her."

I smiled.

He picked up another taco.

"That's two pieces of personal information," I said. "I owe you."

He narrowed his gaze on me. "When was the last time you dated, Ani?"

"The last time I was with someone was before I left L.A., four years ago."

"What did they do to turn you off dating?"

I opened my mouth and nothing came out. Which was awkward.

"It's okay," he said. "You don't have to answer if you don't want to."

"No. No, I'm going to." I took another sip of my drink and got the words straight in my head. "What happened was, I went through some bad times. He got bored of me being down. I wasn't fun anymore, you know? He told me to shake it off."

"What did you do?"

"I shook him off instead."

"Good," he said.

The duet with Grace ended and another song started. Garrett sat back, the tension easing out of him. You could see it in the lines of his face and the set of his broad shoulders. He turned to me and said, "My turn again. Got any questions you want to ask?"

"I think this works best when you choose what you're comfortable telling me."

"You might have a point."

On the dance floor, Magda and her second husband, Ross, were getting down to Aretha Franklin. The smiles on their faces were wide. Garrett watched them in silence for a moment.

"Ross works in logging," I said, nodding at the tall silver-haired man. "He and Magda got married a little over a year after her first husband died in a car accident. I remember the gossip going around town about it at the time."

He nodded.

"She and her first husband had been childhood sweethearts. She was devastated when he died. But then Ross came along and he made her so happy," I said. "It was like she was willing to try living again. To give the world another chance even though it had kicked her in the ass and then some."

For a long moment, he said nothing. "I didn't think I'd ever get married. Nothing against the institution, it just wasn't for me. Settle down and the party stops. Who the hell would want that? Then I met Grace."

The wistful tone in his deep voice made my smile falter. And something sharp and ugly twisted inside of my chest. I was jealous of a dead woman. How fucked up was that?

"What about you?"

"Um. Yeah, no. I won't even date, so I'm thinking the chances of marital bliss are pretty slim."

"Hmm." His gaze slid over me again. "You look nice, Ani. But then you always look nice."

"Thank you." I tried smiling again. "Actually, I do have a question for you."

"Shoot."

"I know you said something about Grace liking the idea of Wildwood for your retirement or whatever. But why did you decide to come here after your travels?"

He sighed. "The answer is involved."

I just waited and let him decide if he wanted to talk about it or not.

"It took a while to accept she was gone. Then even longer to figure out a way to be here without her. Something like that happens and you know life is never going to be the same again. But eventually it might be different and okay. Being in places where she hadn't been seemed easier."

"She never came to see the house?"

"Nope," he said. "The house was her dream of a quiet life for us. Away from work and L.A. and everything. She wanted a big old Victorian surrounded by trees and mountains. Bought it based on photos alone. It occurred to me that it might be a good place for me to hole up for a while. Then Smith came up and brought Gene with him and invited you over . . . and here we are."

My smile was gentle as I tapped my glass against his. "Cheers, friend."

"Cheers. One of these days we're going to manage to have a conversation that doesn't wind up being deep." He picked up his drink. "We'll talk about stupid irreverent shit that requires no soul searching and doesn't matter. In the meantime, how about a game of pool?"

"Sounds good," I said. "But be warned. They're respecting your privacy and keeping their distance while we're in this booth. If we go out there, however, I can guarantee everyone is going to want to meet you. Are you ready for that?"

He took a deep breath and let it out slowly. "Let's find out."

Chapter Seven

THE INEVITABLE HAPPENED MONDAY MORNING AT A quarter past ten. A woman around my age with cool bangs and a designer purse came into the general store with an amiable smile on her face and her cell in her hand. "Hey there. I'm looking for a friend of mine named Garrett. He moved to the area recently."

"Oh," was my super-smart reply.

"I was just passing through and thought I'd stop by. But my cell isn't working and I can't find his address," she said. "It's such a small town. I don't suppose you know where he lives?"

"You were just passing through?" I asked with some skepticism. Which was valid given the town was located right smack bang between nowhere and nothing.

"That's right."

"Garrett, did you say?" Linda kept right on shuffling her tarot cards. "Have you heard of anyone by that name, Ani?"

I shook my head and feigned much sadness. "No. Sorry."

"Damn," said the stranger. "Are you sure? I heard he was here."

Emma wandered in with a Bloody Mary in her hand. "Sorry about the wait, Linda."

"Thank you, sweetie. Much appreciated." Linda didn't always start the day with a pot of tea. It depended on her mood and the amount of red wine consumed the night before. She took a bite out of the decorative celery stalk. "So you said you're a journalist? How wonderful. That must be a fascinating career."

"What?" The woman's brows arched. "No. I never said that. I mean—"

"I could have sworn I'd seen you on one of those celebrity gossip shows," mused Linda.

Emma cocked her head. "You really do look familiar. Are you sure you're not a reporter?"

All trace of the smile disappeared. "I know he's here. You might as well just tell me."

"Who were we talking about again?" I asked.

"Garrett from The Dead Heart," our visitor ground out through clenched teeth. "How much do you want?"

"You mean like money?"

"Yes. I need his address. What'll it take?"

I shook my head. "If someone famous was in town, don't you think I'd already have his face on tea towels and coffee mugs ready to sell to tourists?"

"And like maps to his house," enthused Emma. "I bet we could sell those for at least a couple of bucks apiece."

"I don't know if you noticed, but this town is kind of dying," I said. "We definitely couldn't afford to pass up an opportunity like that."

Doubt crossed the reporter's face.

"What have you been told, exactly?"

"I wish he *had* moved to town. Nothing ever happens around here," said Emma with a dramatic tug of her black braid. "It's how I got pregnant. There was nothing better to do."

"Things have been a little slow around here for the last fifty years or so. That's true. But I'm sure it'll pick up any day now." Linda sighed. "I don't know why you think this Garrett fellow might be here, but I'm afraid you've been misled. You're right, this is a small place. And someone new and exciting like that would not escape my notice."

I gave my own braid a tug. "It would be nice to have something new to talk about. Rehashing the events of the fire of 1921 is getting a bit old."

"But he sent me pictures of him jogging down Main Street." The woman frowned, reaching for her cell. "I suppose they could be fake."

"Who is *he*?" I asked. "If you don't mind me asking."

She didn't even hesitate. So much for not revealing sources. "He said his name was Christian."

I wrinkled my nose. "Christian?"

"Oh, that boy," said Linda. "He's always causing trouble. Just last year he got caught tipping cows. And at the age of twenty-nine, if you can you believe it?"

"Then there was the time he drove a tractor into the river," I added helpfully.

Emma nodded. "Mr. Carmichael is still furious about that."

The woman's brows crept higher and higher.

Josh walked in and held up two fingers. I got busy making his coffee.

91

"You haven't met anyone new in town by the name of Garrett, have you?" asked the reporter. "He's the lead singer from the band The Dead Heart."

Josh took off his cap and smoothed down his mullet. He really was proud of his hair. "A rock band?"

"That's right."

"I don't listen to that nonsense."

The woman visibly deflated. As you would if you'd driven all the way up here for the scoop of the century regarding a missing rock star and thought you'd been misled. Without another word, she stomped out of the general store.

Me: Reporter in town. Stay hidden.

Garrett: Shit. Ok.

Me: Situation is under control. I think.

Worried glances were exchanged as Emma peeked out the front door. "She's heading over to the bar. Yong will handle her. He knows the deal."

"Christian still working out at the Miller farm?" I asked, untying my apron.

Linda nodded.

"He'll be over at the bar later," said Emma. "You may as well wait. We'll outnumber him and there'll be fewer places for him to run and hide."

"I needed the money," whined Christian. "It was nothing personal."

True to our word, Emma and I had him cornered in the

bar soon after five. There was real fear in his eyes. Christian had floppy blond hair and dimples renowned wide and far for winning over the ladies. No joke. He'd actually won best shit-eating grin at the county fair a few years back. But his trademark smirk wasn't working this time.

Emma waved her broom in a threatening manner. "Trust me when I tell you that screwing someone over is always personal. How could you do that to Garrett? After everything he's been through?"

"Oh, yeah. We should definitely feel bad for the millionaire." Christian held up his hands. "Yong, man, tell your woman to calm down, would you?"

"Not a chance," muttered Yong.

Emma blew him a kiss.

"He's a part of our community," I said. "We help each other here. Or did you miss that memo?"

"Ani, c'mon," pleaded Christian. "You really want to hang out with some asshole who thinks he's better than us?"

I shook my head. "You don't even know him. Stop being an ass."

"All right, that's enough," said Yong. "You're banned from the bar for a month."

"What!?" Christian proceeded to throw a tantrum. "No way. Come on, man!"

"Get out of here before my wife disembowels you with a broom. I don't want to have to clean that mess off the floor."

Christian stomped his way to the door. "This is fucked. Chad said no one would care even if they did find out. It was just meant to be easy money."

"Wait!" I hollered. "What exactly does Chad have to do with this?"

"The dude that was doing his best to fall into your cleavage?" asked Garrett later that night.

When I arrived home he was outside with Gene, so we were talking through the fence between our properties. Overhead, the sky was heavy with clouds, the stars only peeking out now and then, and fireflies moved amongst the tall pines. Gene sniffed at various spots on the ground when he wasn't playing with a length of knotted rope.

"No he wasn't," I said.

"Christian? The one who kept grinning at everything, right?"

"Right."

The man said nothing. He just crossed his arms and stared at me. A favorite pose of his and one I immensely appreciated. It accentuated his biceps just so, which was lovely. But the look he was giving me—both stern and brooding at the same time—did not affect my nether regions at all. Because we were *just friends*.

"If he was, I don't care and I didn't notice," I said, a touch defensively for some reason.

"You're allowed to objectify me, but I'm not supposed to notice when some asshole is all over you?"

"You know I deleted the picture of you off my cell. And how was he all over me?"

"The hug he gave you at the pool table."

I groaned. "Christian operates under the delusion that he's the town heartthrob. But, I assure you, he is not. The fact that Chad was involved, however, interests me greatly."

"Who is Chad?" he asked.

"My ex."

He frowned. "The one you shook off in L.A.?"

"Yeah. We all went to school together. Then Chad and I were both in L.A. after college. We met up for a drink and the rest is history. Guess Christian and he are still in contact."

"You don't talk to him?"

"Heck no. He was horrible to me at the end. Why would I?" I asked. "At any rate, they were texting, and Chad talked Christian into contacting the reporter and trying to sell some shots of you, along with information regarding your whereabouts. But we convinced the reporter that he was a simple-minded swindler and not to be trusted. It would seem you're safe for now."

"Okay."

"Yeah." I sighed. "This is why we can't have nice things."

Garrett cocked his head. "Am I the nice thing in his scenario?"

"The size of the ego on you. Why, it's awe-inspiring."

The edge of his mouth inched up just a little. Then it was gone. "Do you think your ex wants you back?"

"No, of course not. He's just causing trouble," I explained. "He comes back to town about once a year for the holidays and we're coldly polite to each other, as the season dictates. The last his aunt told me, he was dating some wealthy influencer type who sells crystal eggs for people to insert into themselves. It's all about spiritual transformation through strengthening of the vaginal muscles, apparently."

"Huh."

"And you can set aside your weird belief that anyone in the

nearby vicinity is interested in getting into my pants. I assure you, they are not."

"Why?"

I sighed. "It's a small town, Garrett. I played spin the bottle and made out in closets with everyone of an appropriate age over a decade ago. Not to mention all of the late-night skinny-dipping in the river. We all know way too much about each other to find anyone alluring. No one is harboring any secret crushes."

He just nodded.

"Am I allowed to ask why you care?"

"Seems we're both working on getting past some things. Guess I'm interested to see if breaking your no-dating rule is one of those things."

I took a step closer, hanging onto the strap of my cross-body purse. The moon hung low in the distance, barely clearing the sharp tips of the iron palings in his people-proof fence. "If I dip my toe back into the dating pool, will you?"

"No." He stared at my shoes for a minute. At least, he seemed to be staring in that general vicinity. But I doubt he could tell their color in the dark and his face betrayed nothing. "I have to head down to L.A. tomorrow to see to a few things. I'll be back in a few days."

"Or maybe you'll like being back in the big city with all your old friends so much that you'll stay. You never know, it could happen."

Nothing from him.

"Are you going to be okay?" I asked. Though I should have kept my mouth shut. "It's the first time you've been back in a couple of years, isn't it?"

"Yeah."

"It'll probably stir up a lot of old memories."

He turned his face away. The lights from the house behind him limned him in a faint gold. And the I-don't-want-to-talk-about-this vibes coming off the man were intense. "I'll be fine."

"Did you want me to look after Gene?"

"No. Thanks. I'm taking him with me."

"At least you won't be alone," I said, taking a step back and raising my hand in farewell. "Safe travels."

"Ani . . ."

"Hmm?"

"I, ah . . . nothing." He hung his head and gripped the back of his neck. "Have a good week, yeah?"

Then he turned and walked away.

For most of the four years back in Wildwood, living without dick had been no big deal. I could see to my own needs just fine. Though my libido had been on an extended vacation for various reasons. Let's not question why it chose to come roaring back to life now. I wasn't ready to face the way-too-obvious answer.

The lack of lights on over at Garrett's house made my corner of the world seem lonely. I used to like the quiet. The way I could look out my front window and see anyone coming from a mile away because I was the only person down this end of the street. With his absence, however, my whole world felt . . . off. Which was ridiculous. He'd been gone for a grand total of two whole days. Talk about being a drama queen.

I did not miss Garrett. I was just in a mood or something. Maybe I was about to get my period. Or I could still be processing our crushing defeat at trivia the night before. Linda said we took it far too seriously and declined to join us next week. The Matriarchy Monsters were therefore still down a member. Not great.

My general rule was that I didn't use my porch after sunset. Routine dictated that I be safely locked up inside by then. Or be surrounded with friends at the bar or some other venue. Any coming and going was done in a swift and safe fashion. All vehicle doors locked and a can of mace in my purse. It really was a wonder Smith hadn't copped a face full of pepper spray the night he'd come in search of a corkscrew.

But back to the porch. Maria and Cézanne had helped me decorate it soon after I bought the place. I focused on the old Adirondack chairs, colorful cushions, and potted plants while they strung up party lights and placed pillar candles around. The only times the lights and candles were used were when they decided we should take our drinks outside and enjoy the night. But the tiny green lights of fireflies were flitting about in the woods. I fucking loved fireflies. Guess they reminded me of my childhood.

I weighed the glass of red from Cézanne's winery in my hand. A grown-ass woman could sit on her porch. It shouldn't matter that the sun had been down for hours. I could be brave. I could do this. There were no boogeymen or unnamed terrors waiting behind the bushes. Nothing would pounce. If Garrett could face his fears and go back to L.A., then I could step outside my own damn front door. Surely. Though taking my can of mace with me wasn't a bad idea. Just in case.

My heart hammered inside my chest, but it was easily ignored. I settled on a chair and took deep, even breaths. The only sounds were the bugs going hard at it and a breeze blowing through the pines. Everything was peaceful. Everything was still.

I took a sip of wine and waited for the panic to pass. And it would. Eventually. While I would never be a hiking, rafting, rock-climbing type, I could experience more of the goodness Wildwood had to offer right here. I didn't have to hide behind a locked door all of my life.

When my hands wouldn't stop shaking, I set the glass of wine aside and put the mace in my lap. Distracting myself might be a smart idea.

Since the rock star had moved in next door, I'd avoided watching music videos or reading celebrity gossip. It seemed wrong somehow. And the man in those videos seemed a separate entity from the Garrett I knew. He was performing, playing it up for the camera, being the showman. Much as he'd explained to me soon after we met. It wasn't really him.

Those weren't the only ways in which he seemed different in those videos. There were fewer lines on his face. No trace of heartbreak or world-weariness. None of the sorrow in his eyes. He didn't seem distant, subdued, or just plain older in the way he did now.

In the way that I knew him.

At any rate, curiosity was a terrible thing and in the absence of my neighbor, I went looking for him online. And holy shit, was he present. There were shots of him getting out of his black Range Rover with Gene in tow outside a sprawling white mansion in the hills. Sunglasses and a ball cap hid most of his face. An article speculated on what his return to L.A. might mean. Were The Dead Heart getting back together?

This was followed by shots of him and Smith chatting on a

balcony. Must have been taken with a long-range lens. The conversation didn't seem to be a happy one, given their body language. No wonder he wanted to get away from the city. Living your life under a microscope like this would suck. Too many people paying me attention after my mini makeover had pissed me off. This, however, was on a whole other level.

The next photos were taken at night as he walked into a bar. Garrett was wearing a black leather jacket and had his face partly turned away from the camera. He was holding hands with a lithe, glamorous blonde in a sleek designer dress. They looked good together. Real good. Like they belonged.

Garrett and I were just friends, so I should be happy that he was out and enjoying himself instead of hiding away at home, obsessing about his dead wife and dwelling on the past. I *would* be happy for him. Any moment now. Because he'd been through so much and he deserved good things.

None of this, however, explained why I wanted to cry.

Chapter Eight

I T STARTED BRIGHT AND EARLY. AS SOON AS I OPENED THE general store doors, in fact. The walkers stormed in wearing their usual array of tight-fitting workout gear. How you could appear put together while sweating was a mystery to me. With my hair in a ponytail and basic makeup accompanied by a whole lot of concealer, I still looked like I hadn't gotten any sleep. Because sometimes life sucks.

"Ladies," I said, taking shelter behind the counter. "How can I help you this morning?"

The lead walker brandished her cell at me with that photo on the screen. "I can't believe he would do this to you."

"After you going out of your way to make him feel welcome here," said the second.

"Well, all of us did, really," added the third. "I made him my pie."

I kept my mouth shut.

"You two looked so close at Margarita Night," said the first.

The second nodded. "We were sensing distinct romantic possibilities."

"And now here we are," lamented the third. "Talk about disappointed."

"He told us at the bar that he wants to make a life away from all of that nonsense," said the first.

The second shrugged. "There's not that many single people in town."

"And you're definitely one of the better choices," stated the third. "He's going to regret this. You won't see me baking for that man again."

"This is quite kind of you all," I said, bemused. "Along with being low-level embarrassing. But Garrett and I are not and have never been together, and he doesn't owe me anything. Really."

One by one, they all gave me a knowing sad smile. Then off they went to march their usual circuit around town.

Huh. Guess there wasn't anyone who hadn't been disappointed in love a time or two. Not that I was in love with him, because that would be stupid. I had barely begun to acknowledge that I might even have any deeper feelings for him. Hands down, the heart was the most foolish organ in the human body.

The truth was, he belonged with the twenty-one-year-old blond model from the photo. She of the designer dress and pert tits. Mine were too heavy for any of that nonsense and had a tendency to get away from me without underwire. And let's not even discuss my ass or thighs. Liking Garrett in any way outside of friendship had been nothing more than a fever dream. And now it was over.

I took a sip of coffee and raised my hand as Claude walked in the door, followed by Cézanne and Linda. *Shit.*

"Why are you all here?" I asked. "Apart from you, Claude. I can smell the pecan pie. Yum."

He set the selection of boxes down on the counter. "I'll have an espresso when you're ready."

I gave him a smile. "You got it."

"You turned off your cell," said Cézanne. "We're assuming it's because you were avoiding something. But in the process, you worried the crap out of all of your friends."

"Dammit. Hang on." I rushed out back to grab the offending item out of my purse. And sure enough, there was a mess of texts, voice messages, and missed calls. All of which revolved around Garrett and the photo. "Here's the thing," I said, heading back out front. "I don't want to talk about it. Because there is nothing to talk about."

"But you have feelings for him." Linda hammered her fist on the counter in a sudden outburst of passion. "Goodness gracious, young lady. Own your emotions. Take pride in your heart. Never be ashamed to care about someone."

"I don't . . . We're just friends."

Cézanne made an indelicate noise. "Please. We know you. You don't think we can tell when someone finally makes you wake up and pay attention again?"

"It was pretty obvious you were sweet on him, Ani," said Claude. "I'm sorry it didn't work out."

"He's a rich and famous rock star, and I'm me. It was never going to happen. I mean, the man could date anyone he wants." I groaned. "How do you all even know about it at this hour? None of you have a great interest in celebrity gossip. Apart from Cézanne's Pete Davidson fascination, which I share."

"Josh saw it on the entertainment news channel late last

night and activated the phone tree," said Linda. "He'd be here now, but Mayor Carmichael's truck broke down just out of town. Emma and Yong are busy with a sick baby, but send their love. And Magda and Ross are down at her sister's place in Sacramento and wish you all the best."

"What Ross actually said was that he hopes the rock star falls off the face of the earth, never to be seen again," said Claude. "But he's just hurting. You know how he loves a wedding."

"Give me strength," I whispered. "We're just friends."

All three of them gave me knowing looks. Ugh.

"Everyone knows and you've all been discussing it?" I asked.

Cézanne nodded. "Don't pretend to be surprised. You knew what this town was like when you moved back here."

I ever so subtly banged my forehead against the counter a couple of times. It didn't help.

"Ani," said Linda, rubbing my back. Her collection of silver bangles jingling all the while. "I'm sorry Neptune is creating chaos around relationships this month. But is it so difficult to accept that you are loved? That we want your hopes and dreams to come true?"

"You all have to promise not to say anything to him." I straightened and stared them each in the eye. "It's embarrassing enough that you've all been talking about it behind my back."

"Well, now . . ." Claude pinched his lips between his fingers.

"Claude," I admonished. "Promise me. Please."

"Oh, all right then. But he could do with someone sitting him down and having a serious man-to-man talk."

"Don't look at me," said Cézanne. "You know I'll behave. Though I'd dearly love to knee him in the nuts for you."

I snorted. "The sentiment is appreciated."

"Whatever you say, dear," said Linda. "I'll communicate your wishes to the group chat."

"Thank you." I relaxed a little. "Really. Thank you for caring. Now let's never talk about it ever again."

A storm rolled in Saturday afternoon along with my neighbor. Twilight was coming on quickly, care of the gray sky. I watched his Range Rover drive through the muddy puddles on our road, pause at the security gate, then head on inside. And I did all of this hiding behind my curtain like a creeper, because apparently that's where I was at in life.

My week post–news of the photos hitting the internet had been average. I comfort-ate half a pecan pie and binged several seasons of *Schitt's Creek*. The ones with Patrick in them. But not even he and David and their love story could make me smile.

And now Garrett was home. Okay. But wait . . .

All of a sudden, a large dark object zoomed up my neighbor's driveway, only just clearing the security gates before they would have slammed shut on his tail. Gene had made a break for it. His intended destination was soon made clear as his wet paws skidded across my front porch. Next, he commenced singing the song of his people. Holy shit, the dog could howl.

"Hey, Gene," I said, fumbling with the locks on my front door before throwing it open. "Hello, beautiful boy. What's all the fuss about, huh?"

After giving me a doggy grin, he shook himself dry, wetting me from head to toe in the process. Meanwhile, Garrett stood in the rain, waiting for the security gates to open so he could come after his pooch. Awesome.

Guess I had to get this awkward reunion over and done with sometime. It's not like anything had actually changed in our relationship. I remained the safe friend, et cetera. Seeing as I was already damp care of Gene, I slid my fingers under his collar and started walking him home. My blue jeans and white tank top were drenched in no time. "Lose something?"

"Yeah. Guess he missed you," said Garrett, shoving his hand through his dark wet hair. Of course, wet looked good on him. It was like he was in the middle of making an ad for designer cologne. As if any moment now he'd pull out an electric guitar and perform a solo. "Thanks."

And the warm smile he gave me . . . he had no business looking at me like that. None at all. His gaze dipped to the white lace bra visible through my wet tank before jumping back to my face. Then his jaw firmed and he asked, "How have you been?"

"Good. Great. And you?"

"Fine," he said, taking charge of his dog. "Glad to be back. Hell of a drive."

I smiled. "Yeah."

He immediately narrowed his eyes on me. "What's wrong?"

"Nothing. We can talk later. I'll let you get in out of the rain."

"Hang on," he said, grabbing hold of my arm. His hand was large and warm and felt altogether too good and grounding, given the situation. "Ani, why are you giving me your fake smile?"

Thunder rolled far off in the distance and the rain came down harder.

"I'm not giving you a fake smile."

"Yeah, you are. You're also avoiding looking me in the eye."

He paused and frowned. "You've seen those pictures, haven't you?"

"I, um . . . It's none of my business."

Gene tugged and Garrett let him go. The dog immediately dropping and rolling in the nearest puddle of muddy water. Talk about living your best life.

"I mean, it's great that you went out and had some fun," I said. "This is ridiculous. We're both soaked. I'm going to head inside."

His grip on me tightened. It was firm, but not painful. "Wait a minute, Ani. Let me explain."

"You don't need to ex—"

"Smith wouldn't get off my case about going out. So I agreed to go to the opening of a new nightclub by a friend of ours." He took a step closer so he wouldn't have to yell over the weather. "Smith invited the woman he's dating, and she invited her friend. And the friend was wearing these fancy high heels and almost tripped getting out of the car. I grabbed her hand to stop her from falling. Then the paparazzi freaked her out and she was clinging to me, so I just focused on getting her inside. That's when they took those photos."

"She was very beautiful."

"She was very young," he said. "And you're still angry."

"I'm not angry. I'm glad you got out and spent some time with your friend. But all of this . . . it's still none of my business. We're just friends." I attempted to step back, and his frown increased to a scowl. "Garrett, seriously, it's fine. Can you let go of me now, please?"

"If it's so fucking fine, then why the hell do I feel this overwhelming need to explain myself to you?" His forehead was a mess of furrowed lines. And he was more than willing to get all up in my face about the matter. "Can you tell me that much?"

"I don't know!"

"Me neither!" he yelled straight back. "Shit."

I wiped the rain out of my eyes. "This is stupid. Let's talk about this later when we've both had a chance to get dry and you've had some sleep and—"

His spare hand slipped around the back of my neck to take hold of me and his mouth was on mine. *Holy shit.* Garrett was kissing me. There was no lead-in or warning. Just his firm, warm lips and the tease of his tongue slipping into my mouth.

I went from attempting to establish some physical and emotional distance between us (for the sake of my own sanity) to making out with him on his front lawn in the rain. Because it never even occurred to me not to kiss him back or to try to stop things. I was drowning in him. The heat and demand and everything. He was everything. I anchored myself to him with a fistful of his shirt and held on for dear life. The heat spreading through my veins was so foreign. It had been a long time since I'd felt anything like this. And I was so desperate for his touch and attention, if he took it away from me now I might cry.

But then he stepped back, his hands falling to his sides, and his blue eyes wide with both horror and regret. Just great. The way the expression on his face sucked any hope or joy right out of my life.

"Garrett."

"Fuck," was all he said. Then he turned and headed for the open gate with a muddy Gene at his heels. And I stood there and watched him go.

Me: I'm here whenever you're ready to talk.

"He kissed you in the rain, then freaked out and ran away?" asked Cézanne. "Seriously?"

I nodded and continued sorting through the sales rack at a cool little boutique we'd found in Falls Creek. Makeovers required stuff. Magda sold an organic range of makeup and hair products. But not living in tees and jeans or leggings constantly required an actual trip out of town. And my current bad mood due to a certain man required retail therapy.

Sunday was a busy day in Falls Creek. Lots of tourists. They wandered in and out of the shops and restaurants with smiles on their faces. As much as I'd love to see this sort of interest in Wildwood, I had no idea how to make it happen. It would take resources, and our township had next to none.

"You made a grown man run away in fear." Cézanne shook her head. "Impressive."

"The terror and shame on his face was a lot," I said, holding up a floral gray-and-white sleeveless cotton top with a button front and beautiful tie-waist feature. "What about this?"

"Nice. It's reduced because there's a spot of lipstick on the collar. But you can blot that off with some rubbing alcohol."

"I tried texting him last night, but nada."

"Maybe he just needs time to process the experience and his feelings before sitting down with you and talking it through."

I gave her a look. "You don't believe that."

"It would be nice, though, wouldn't it?" She sighed. "How are you holding up?"

"I can't compete with Grace." I shrugged. "She was basically superhuman. Beautiful and amazing and talented. I'm not being down on myself. It's just the truth."

"You are sort of being down on yourself."

"Maybe a little. But you can see where I'm coming from."

"You're beautiful and amazing and talented too in your own way."

"Aw. Thanks, Mom." I grinned and dodged as she aimed an elbow at me. "But he's not ready. I'm not even sure if *I'm* ready."

She passed me a navy ruffled square-neck sleeveless top. "Try this on. It's a good price and you have great breasts."

"Are you going to try anything?"

"No."

I just waited.

"I'm pregnant," she admitted with a smile.

And I smiled back at her.

She smacked me on the arm. "You knew? Ani, how did you know?"

"Like you weren't sipping water at Margarita Night and avoiding the soft cheese at the winery tasting I helped you with last Saturday."

"Why didn't you say something?"

"Because it's your choice when to tell people," I said. "Or if you tell them at all. And I could have been wrong. You could have been changing your eating habits for whatever reason. But I'm delighted you're having a baby. Can I be nosy and ask how far along you are?"

"Nine weeks. Still early days. But I'm so happy, and Mike is just over the moon."

"Good." I gave her a hug. "You two are going to be great parents."

"But this is a big-ass change, and you hate change."

I shrugged. "Maybe change isn't so bad. The fact is, regardless of how I feel about it, I can't stop it because the world keeps turning. And change like this, you making a mini you, that's all sorts of awesome. The world needs more of you."

"Thank you. You're going to be a good aunt." She pulled a pair of khaki utility pants off a nearby shelf. "Try these. There's a small hole in the butt of the leggings you're wearing."

"A new pair of pants it is!"

The AC died just after one in the morning on Tuesday. I had been meaning to replace the old unit. However, recent purchases of a new secondhand vehicle and an update to my wardrobe and makeup had delayed things. My father would have given me a stern lecture on my priorities, but oh well.

Of course, each door and window in the cabin was locked tight. I had let myself double-check the fact only twice. As per the advice of the therapist I'd seen way back when, I was attempting to set limits on my obsessive behavior and learning how to build trust in myself. Which also meant, in no time at all, the cabin would be hot, muggy, and all-round hellish.

Swearing hadn't helped. And there was no way I was going to call my friends at this hour and ask if anyone had a fan I could borrow. Also, even if I did, it would only be circulating hot air. I needed to open the windows in the bedroom at the very least.

Mom and Dad had gifted me security screens when I bought the place. They were the reinforced wire ones that couldn't be kicked in or cut with a knife. Therefore, opening the windows shouldn't be a big deal. But of course it was, because I had already broken out in a cold sweat at just the thought. Not good. A spare can of mace sat in my bedside drawer. My cell was nearby if I needed to call for help. I only had to silence the fear and negativity inside my head. Much easier said than done.

"You can do this," I said to myself in an almost calm voice. "Also, you need to get your ass back to therapy if you're serious about dealing with this shit."

Being right could be such a bitch. I was just the worst sometimes.

I breathed in slowly through my nose and out through my mouth. Then I wiggled my fingers and toes and counted backwards from one hundred. All great distractions and much better than having a meltdown.

"Okay," I said finally.

Slow and steady, I turned the key in the lock and pushed the window open. Cool air rushed in, which was gratifying as fuck. I took a step back and waited for disaster to occur. For a monster to leap out at me or whatever.

Then I heard something. A truly amazing something. Along with the usual sounds of the distant river and the woods at night came the soft strains of a guitar. Soon it was accompanied by a familiar voice. I didn't recognize the song, but he had said he was working on new music. Whatever it was, it was beautiful.

With a lot less fuss, I unlocked and opened the second bedroom window. The one facing his house. Curiosity could occasionally beat panic, apparently. This window was much better. I could hear the notes of the guitar more clearly, the hum and growl of his voice. And it all soothed me no end. I lay down on my bed in the dark and listened.

Since our disastrous, dramatic kiss in the rain two days ago, there'd been nothing but silence. Which hurt. It should be harder to ghost a neighbor. But here we were. There were still lots of good things in my life. Such as friends and family, box mac and cheese with truffle oil, and a wonderful selection of romance novels waiting for me by the bed. I lived a full life. Just because he apparently no longer wanted to be a part of it didn't mean I was going to fall apart or some such shit.

My neighbor might well have feelings for me. But there was nothing I could do about that. His grief would take as long as was necessary. He might never be ready or interested in moving on. And as his friend, or former friend as the case may be, respecting his decision and giving him the space he wanted was the right thing to do. At least this way, with the windows open, I could still hear him. Not just a recording, but the real him. Guess it was better than nothing.

Chapter Nine

A SURPRISING NUMBER OF PEOPLE WERE ON MAIN STREET on Wednesday morning. Lots of trucks, too. It was quite possibly the first traffic jam in the history of Wildwood. Signs on the various vehicles read plumber, builder, electrician, and so on. And they were walking in and out of all the empty buildings, along with the neglected theater and diner. Something was most definitely afoot.

Which was good. I could do with something to distract me from the absence of a certain someone.

"What the hell?" I mumbled as Linda joined me on the sidewalk.

"I have no idea," she said with no small amount of wonder. "Why don't you go and ask?"

I shoved my hands in the pockets of my black waist apron. It complemented my blue jeans and white tank and pale blue Chucks just fine. While the winged eyeliner might be a little fancy for work, I did not care. I was feeling myself. It was all good. And one of these days I was going to attempt space buns.

Why should Josh be the only person in these parts who had fun with his hair?

"Be sure to tell them the first coffee is half price," said Linda. "And that we have fresh doughnuts and pastries daily."

"Did Mayor Carmichael say anything about this?"

"He's actually been absent from church the last few Sundays. Something about his hip playing up," she said. "But it's not as if he has any real interest in what's happening. The only reason he's still mayor is no one can be bothered running against him and he likes having the title."

"This is true."

She gave me a nudge. "Go and get the gossip, Ani. I've got the store."

A passing tradesperson told me the new owner of the buildings was in the diner. It seemed safest to go straight to the source. No messing around with maybes.

As far as I knew, Eileen had yet to find anyone interested in buying the place since she closed up shop and retired to Florida. Guess that had changed. Three years could make for a lot of dust. But the black-and-white-checked laminate floor, metal-edged tables, and turquoise booths held so many memories. Dad and I used to stop by for a burger and fries every Saturday. Mom liked to take her time at the farmers' market in Falls Creek and Dad hated shopping. My teenage self, on the other hand, enjoyed shopping, just not when it consisted largely of fresh produce. To think of all the conversations Dad and I had in this space.

But back to the here and now. Studying an array of papers spread across the counter stood Claude, Lupita, and Garrett. And I stopped dead at the sight. It was a small town, so we couldn't avoid each other forever. Though a few more days without the rock star would have been nice. A chance to practice my indifference and put my feelings back in a box.

After all, I neither needed nor wanted a man in my life. There'd been enough changes lately, what with me putting effort into my appearance and pushing at the boundaries of my fears. I'd started sitting outside with a book at night and sleeping with the bedroom windows open. It was more than enough.

"Excuse me, miss," said a dude carrying a toolbox.

I stepped inside. "Sorry."

"Ani, come on in." Claude's smile was wide. "We're reopening the diner. Isn't it exciting?"

"Wow."

Lupita smacked a kiss on my cheek, then wiped her lipstick off my face with the pad of her thumb. "I'm going to make my breakfast burritos."

"We'll have pancakes, burgers, sandwiches, and salads, too," said Claude. "My nephew is moving out from Chicago to help."

I smiled. "That's amazing."

"Garrett's just about bought up the whole damn town. He says he's going to bring it back to life."

And all the while, the rock star stood there, frowned at me, and said nothing. Like an asshole. I don't think it had occurred to me to be angry about what happened between us before then. But I sure as hell was now.

"Can we talk out back for a second, please?" I asked, and led the way to the kitchen.

Pots and pans sat abandoned on the grill and the scent of fried food still lingered in the air. Eileen had owned the place for as long as I could remember. And her father before her. It tended to often be the way in small towns. How things got handed down through families.

"I'd forgotten how much I used to love this place," I said, taking it all in. "How much I've missed it."

Garrett leaned a hip against the old counter and stared down at me. Of course he also had his arms crossed, because being defensive and withdrawn was his chosen aesthetic. "What's up?"

"Try again," I snapped.

A little muscle in his jaw went pop. His gaze dipped, then he caught himself and most definitely did not look at the color of my shoes. Lucky for him, given my current mood.

"You seem to need some help now and then with being a friend. So consider this me helping you," I said. "You can pretend you never kissed me, but you do not get to pretend I don't exist."

He sighed. "I'm sorry."

"Keep going."

"It was a mistake. It never should have happened. I had no business . . ."

"Kissing me?" Despite anticipating this line of defense, it still hurt like hell. Kind of like when Brittany Daly tripped me and knocked the wind out of me in fourth grade. As I recall, that was about a boy too. "Okay. Thank you, Garrett. Apology accepted."

His brows rose. "You're all right with that? With me saying it was a mistake?"

"Why wouldn't I be?"

"Ah, no reason. That's . . . yeah, that's great. So we can just go back to the way things were before?"

"Yes."

"Good."

I nodded. "Now that we have that sorted, what are you doing to my town, Garrett?"

"It was you who actually gave me the idea," he said. "Telling me about the guy who raised the rent and drove all of those people out of business. I got my lawyer to track him down and make him an offer. The man couldn't offload the properties fast enough. He even agreed to rush things and let us get in here early to start."

"I don't doubt he was keen. The idiot is making no income while paying taxes. But what's in it for you?"

"After I signed the contract for the sale of the West Hollywood house, I got to thinking. That part of my life is finished. But I don't want to go back to aimlessly wandering around," he said. "It's time to start something new. I like it here in Wildwood and I plan on staying and making it my home."

"Okay."

"Emma was telling me what you said to that reporter. About how you'd use me being here to make money."

"Garrett, I didn't—"

"I know you didn't mean it," he said. "But maybe you should. Sooner or later it's going to get out that I'm here. What if we prepare for it and use it to the town's advantage?"

I blew out a breath and thought it over. "That's a huge commitment on your part."

"I've got the cash and I might as well be doing something with it. Something to benefit all of us."

"How did you get things moving so quickly?"

"Money," he said. "Tell me what you think."

"I mean, it's a dream come true. I just don't want you changing your mind and winding up regretting it. Taking on too much or whatever."

"That's not going to happen," he said. Then the most amazing thing occurred . . . the man actually smiled. And oh God, it was beautiful, the happiness in his eyes. "You should see the plans that are getting drawn up. The ideas we have. I asked Claude and Lupe to ask around the last couple of days on the quiet, and people want to do things in this town. They want to get back into these places and run their businesses. They want to take pride in their town; they just need a little help."

"You're really into all of this," I said with a smile of my own. "You finally found your way forward."

"Yeah. I guess I did."

"That's great, Garrett. That's really great."

"Thanks." His smile softened. "I'm glad you feel that way. 'Cause I actually need your help with something."

"Order!" Mayor Carmichael banged the gavel. "Sit down, Josh. You've had your say."

The residents of Wildwood crowded into the town hall for an emergency meeting Thursday night. Guess it was to be expected. Some people were so stuck in their ways. They'd rather have the town die a slow death than deal with actual change. And what Garrett had started on Main Street was huge. Mayor Carmichael couldn't be unhappier with all of the plans. Nor the fact that he was required to be present for the meeting.

Which got me thinking. "I have something to say."

The chaos continued.

"I got you!" yelled Cézanne. Then she stuck two fingers in her mouth and let loose with a whistle that worked a treat.

Her husband Mike gave her an adoring smile.

"Ani, stand up, for goodness sake," prodded Linda. "You have the right to your say."

I got to my feet. "It's not change."

"What?" Mayor Carmichael's bushy gray brows drew together. "Miss, you don't have the floor. Sit down."

"No," I said, raising my voice. "We've been here for over an hour and everyone's saying the same damn thing. They either love it or hate it. But those that hate it—you're looking at it the wrong way. What's happening isn't change in the way that you're thinking."

"How so?" asked Josh. "Are you telling me we're not going to get inundated with outsiders?"

"That might happen either way."

"The town is fine as it is," said Harry. "I don't see why we need all of this fuss."

"You've already heard the arguments about local employment and attracting tourism. But I think we've missed the important point in all of this." I turned to give Garrett a brief smile. He stood to the side of the hall, having given his seat up to Miss Therese from the local inn.

"All my life, we've been saying how great things were in Wildwood in the good old days. And that sentiment has only got stronger in the last decade as one business after another has gone bust," I explained. "Remember how wonderful it was when we could get a burger and shake at the diner? How just a couple of summers ago we were able to buy an ice cream on a hot day? Who here is old enough to recall when we didn't have to drive to Falls Creek to use the library, or see the dentist, or—"

"You can't guarantee we'll get those things back," said one of the walkers. The one with the cool long acrylic nails. "And in the meantime, Main Street is a godawful mess."

"I know we're going to be gone soon if we don't do something. Those buildings have sat empty for years. And they're not the only ones in town that no one was interested in buying." I sighed. "Garrett already has a list of people ready to bring our town back to life. To change it back to how it was in the good old days."

"Does that mean he's bringing back the whorehouse?" snickered Christian. "'Cause I'd be down with that."

Another idiot laughed.

Linda reached out and smacked Christian over the back of the head. "Sex workers deserve respect just like any other," she said. "If you can't give it, then keep your mouth shut or you'll be banned from the general store along with the bar and grill."

Christian rubbed at the back of his head. "Aw, Linda. Don't be like that. I was just having fun."

Cézanne got to her feet. "At present, the people who visit the winery usually don't bother stopping in town. They shop and stay in Falls Creek. But we can change that."

"We have the river just like Falls Creek," I said. "We have the hiking trails and fishing and all of that."

"My inn is full for the first time in I don't know how long," added Miss Therese. "There's architects and engineers and all sorts of interesting people staying and spending their money in our town right now."

"I still don't like it," grumbled Mayor Carmichael from his

seat at the front of the room. "We don't need some stranger coming in and taking over."

More than a couple of people nodded in agreement. Dammit.

"The opportunity to start a business in these storefronts is being offered to locals first," said Garrett. "And rent will be kept at a reasonable rate."

Josh remained standing with his hands on his hips. "Look, Gary, you seem like an okay guy. And we were all happy to help keep your being here on the down low. Apart from an idiot or two."

Christian muttered something, which we all ignored.

"But the fact is, you're new to town and we don't know you yet. Buying up the place like this is big," Josh continued. "You could be some trickster out to rob us blind. Lure us into thinking you care about the town and you want to help . . . then, bang. You take all of our hard-earned money and go back to touring with your rock band and making millions of dollars and pumping out music I don't like. Where would Wildwood be then?"

Garrett's brows sat high on his furrowed brow and his mouth opened just a little. But I doubt he knew what to say.

I, for one, would love to know if Josh had eaten one of Linda's cookies before the meeting. But I couldn't ask that. At least not in public. "Josh, what are you going on about? How exactly is he taking your money?"

"I just think we'd all feel a whole hell of a lot better if one of us was . . . what's the word?" Josh snapped his fingers. "Liaising with you. Yeah. If someone was representing the town's interests in all of this and making sure you weren't up to any funny business. No insult intended."

"But you did insult him," I said. "Multiple times. You can't just say 'no insult intended' and pretend it didn't happen."

"She has a point." Yong stood at the back of the hall, holding the baby. "Though it is kind of beside the point."

"Whatever," said Josh with a toss of his mullet. "I nominate Ani to be town liaison. She can work with Gary, keep an eye on him and keep all of us in the loop."

"Huh," said Claude. "Now that's a good idea."

My chin jerked up. "Wait. What?"

Garrett just shrugged.

"That's a great idea." Linda stuck up her hand. "I second the motion."

"I third it," cried a walker.

"Oh, yes," said Miss Therese, waving her handkerchief in the air. "I fourth it."

"But Claude and Lupita are already working with Garrett," I said, somewhat flustered. "Surely they'd be a better choice."

Claude clicked his tongue. "We'll be too busy with the diner, Ani."

"Yeah. But I have a job and—"

"It should be you," finished Claude.

"Yes." Linda nodded. "That would definitely be best."

"I have to agree with them there," said Cézanne. And she even managed to keep a straight face.

Holy shit. Talk about a conspiracy. This whole damn town was full of matchmakers.

"Right. You and Garrett are going to work together. It's decided." Josh nodded his head. "You're doing it."

Mayor Carmichael slammed his gavel down again. "I don't like it!"

"No point her being just the liaison, though, is there?" asked Linda. "She needs a little power. And I think it's high time Wildwood had a mayor who didn't nap through town meetings."

"But the next election isn't for ages," said Harry, scratching his head.

"Um," I said, panicking just a little.

"I only fell asleep a time or two," grouched Mayor Carmichael. "I'm up early with the farm."

"You're busy. I agree," said Linda. "Let someone younger have their turn, Roger. Go on. You know you'd rather be at home with your feet up watching a game. It's past time we joined the twenty-first century and had our first female mayor."

Roger studied his gavel. "I don't know."

"Of course, it's up to you." Linda tapped her chin. "But it sure looks like a lot of work is coming the mayor's way. Librans like you don't do well with change even when it's positive. Are you sure you want to deal with all of this and taking care of the farm too?"

"You've given so much, Roger," said Miss Therese. "Maybe it's time to slow down and have a little peace and quiet."

"Don't you try to sweet-talk me, Therese. I know what you're up to." He pursed his wrinkled lips in contemplation. "Fine. I'll resign. But I've been mayor of this town for twenty-eight years."

"Yeah," interjected Josh. "Because no one else wanted the job."

"Silence." Mayor Carmichael banged his gavel for the last time. "I want a statue erected or a park named after me."

"That can be arranged," said Garrett with nil hesitation.

Mayor Carmichael scowled at me from across the room. Then he said, "You're the Bennet girl, aren't you? Have you got time for these duties what with school and everything?"

I frowned. "I'm thirty, not thirteen."

"What are you doing with your hair in pigtails, then?"

"They're not pigtails, they're space buns."

The outgoing mayor stood, leaving his gavel behind with one last look of longing. "I'm out of here. We'll soon see what kind of mess you all get in without me to guide you. And don't think I'll come back even if you beg!"

Miss Therese blew him a kiss. "Thanks, Rog."

"I . . ." I blinked. "Hang on. This can't be official. What about democratic process? I'd just be the interim mayor until we could hold an election, right?"

"Why waste time? Let me make it official for you." Yong looked around the room. "Anyone else want to be mayor and work with Garrett representing the town and sorting all of this out and answering everybody's annoying questions all of the time and receiving very little thanks and absolutely no monetary compensation?"

Emma laughed. "Hell no."

"She's a sucker," mumbled Josh.

The finger I pointed at him was highly aggressive. "I heard that."

And there were plenty of people shaking their heads and a goodly number of no's.

"Yeah," said Yong. "Me neither. You're it, Ani.

Congratulations. Party at the bar tomorrow night to celebrate our new mayor!" #smh

Garrett waited in the foyer of the old movie theater. A table was once again covered in an array of maps and building plans. There he stood, looking entirely too good for my nerves, in jeans and boots. He even wore a navy button-down with the sleeves rolled up. Like any man's muscular forearms should be displayed in such a wanton manner. "Thought you'd look less shell-shocked by now."

"Sorry to disappoint you."

"Do I call you Madam Mayor or Mayor Bennet or . . ."

"That's what I love about this town, so very many funny people." I took a sip from my bottle of water. Holding it gave my hands something to do. "And I am just delighted to represent you all. Temporarily. Until there can be an official vote."

"Look on the bright side, you didn't have to come up with policies or a campaign or any of that bullshit."

"True," I said. "Don't get me wrong, I appreciate the town's hustle."

"Just never saw yourself as mayor?"

"Not even a little."

"You might have gotten bullied just a bit," he said. "But they trust you."

I smiled. "Yeah. I guess they do."

After finishing her morning pot of tea, Linda had told me to go do some mayoring. I just hoped she didn't mess with the display of reusable feminine hygiene products I had been working on. It was on its way to being a masterpiece.

"No one on any of the building crews has sold you out to the media yet?" I asked.

"They all signed NDAs. But we both know it's going to happen sooner or later," he said. "How was your first day as mayor?"

"I delighted a group of small children by agreeing to swear in their dog as deputy mayor. I, for one, think Fluffy has a great career ahead of her in small-town politics."

His smile was brief, but it counted. Yay, me.

And if I wasn't wholly immune to the man, then I could at least keep a safe distance between us. For the sake of my heart and loins, if nothing else. Neither of us wanted to get involved. We were both in agreement about that. So keeping some space between us was the smart thing to do, given the situation.

"You're really thinking of reopening the theater?" I asked, crossing my arms over my breasts.

"Haven't quite decided. But it makes sense to at least fix it while I've got the workers here."

I nodded. "It's all happening so fast."

"I have a great lawyer. She's persuasive as all hell and has her fingers in all sorts of pies. Her partner's big in the building industry. I told them both that money is no issue."

"Wow."

"Got to spend it all on something. Come look at this," he said, nodding at the building plans on top of the pile. "I want to hear what you think."

I took a couple of steps forward and craned my neck. "This is the foyer?"

"Yeah."

"Looks good. Authentic old-time theater, but not dilapidated and falling down."

"How can you see anything from over there?" he asked, moving aside to make room for me. "Come closer, Ani."

"I'm fine where I am."

He frowned and gave me a long look.

"You want to run through your anticipated timeline for all of this?" I asked. "I'm expecting a lot of questions about traffic, when new stores will begin to open, and so on."

"Sure."

"Miss Therese told me you approached her about developing the riverfront land on her property. Building some cabins and such, like to rent?"

"Sooner or later, someone is going to come in and start building holiday rentals. Why shouldn't Miss Therese get in first since she's already set up for that and she's got the space to expand?"

"True."

"As for parking, I've asked the contractors to leave some area around any open current businesses," he said. "Lupita and Claude are keen to have the diner open at the end of next month. All going well. Having to replace pipes in the old barber shop and haberdashery will slow us down a little. But the three store-fronts across the road are in good repair. All they really need is some paint and polish. I'm hoping to have them opening in a couple of weeks."

I raised my brows. "Okay."

"Of course, we'll see what can be done with offering overtime and bringing in extra crews to bring those dates forward."

"What's the rush?"

"I'm impatient, I know," he said. "I could show you the rest of the plans if you like."

"That's all right. I think I have enough information to start with."

"Okay," he said, and held out his hand for shaking. "Nice doing business with you, Mayor."

And I stood there and stared at his hand like a maniac. One with no social skills. Because us touching . . . that was a bad idea.

"Wasn't it you just the other day who was telling me off for avoiding you?" he asked.

"I'm not avoiding you. I'm keeping a careful distance between us."

"You think that's necessary?"

"You think it's not?"

He scratched at this stubble. "Are you worried I'm going to kiss you again? Because I can assure you that's not going to happen. Ani, it was a—"

"Mistake. I know." I smiled. "Thanks for making time for me, Garrett."

"That's your fake smile."

"I'm not actually convinced you know me well enough to tell when I'm faking it."

"And yet I'm right, aren't I?"

I raised a hand. "Bye."

"This doesn't feel like friends."

"Sure it does. Because there're lots of types of friends. We just happen to be the kind now that give each other a little space. See you at the bar tonight?" I didn't wait for an answer.

Chapter Ten

F RIDAY NIGHT IN THE BAR AND GRILL WAS BUSY AS PER
usual. My inauguration party had been in full swing for an
hour or so. Though I could have done without my junior
high school photo hanging up on the wall alongside an American
flag. Pimples suck. But at least my dyed-blue hair still looked
cool. It had taken many hours and countless packs of hair dye
to get it just the right shade. Mom had been ready to pull out
her own hair by the end.

Regardless of the questionable party decorations, the
townsfolk were eating, drinking, and making merry. Some of
the new-to-town contractors and others were also mingling,
which was nice. For the first hour and a half, I'd shaken hands,
passed on information gathered from my visit with Garrett, and
danced with Harry, Claude, and Josh. Now it was time for me
to rest and recuperate.

Garrett appeared at the end of the booth. "Mind if I sit
down?"

"Go ahead."

"Thanks." He slid in opposite me and wasted no time in saying, "I hurt you when I said it was a mistake, didn't I?"

Ugh. "No one likes to hear they were a mistake. But neither of us are actually looking for something to happen here either."

"When you put it that way, giving each other some space sounds smart."

I nodded.

But we looked at each other and neither of us made a move to separate. Feelings really are the worst. What you soon realize going through life is that there's the smart thing to do and then there's the other option. What the heart wants. And the heart is a foolish thing. I loved spending time with Garrett. It had long since gone beyond being a rock-star-and-fan thing. Because, once he gave you a chance to get to know the real him, you soon found out he was great. Grumpy, but great.

One day in the distant future, when I had my shit sorted, I would meet another man. One who was far less complicated, but looked just as good in an old black tee. Or I wouldn't meet someone, but I would adopt a dog and a cat, and carry on just fine with my life with my furry housemates. With my friends, family, and town.

In the meantime, I sat opposite Garrett and did my best not to think of him standing in the rain, staring at me like I was both his curse and his salvation. Because a moment like that could really fuck with your head. And neither of us needed that. Nope. The truth was, denial was the true hero in this situation.

"Smith said to say congratulations on becoming mayor," he said.

"You've been talking to him?"

"He called. I answered."

"Good for you."

"On the house, Garrett," said Emma, sliding a bottle of beer on the table.

"Thanks, Emma. Say thanks to Yong for me, too."

She gave him a wink and was on her way.

"The cloud that was hanging over you has lifted," I said. "It's lovely to see."

"Like you said, I found a way forward. I'm planning a future and not isolating myself anymore."

"Now say it again without looking quite so disconcerted by the idea."

"It's a lot. But I'm dealing." He leaned forward, resting his forearms on the table. "Tell me something personal. Or aren't we the kind of friends who do that anymore? I mean, shit. If you don't feel comfortable—"

"I thought we were going to start talking about shallow, inconsequential stuff."

His attempt at a smile was halfhearted at best. "We can talk about whatever you want."

"Okay." I took a deep breath. "I've actually been doing some work on myself. Made an appointment with a therapist in Falls Creek. Of course, she can't fit me in for a couple of weeks, but . . ."

"That's great."

"You never did ask what it was all about. Exactly what the big bad thing in my past was. I don't think I ever said thank you for that."

"You'll tell me if you want me to know." He picked at the label on his beer bottle. "If you want to and the time is right. There's no rush."

I pushed my plate of garlic fries his way. "Help yourself, Garrett. Don't make me the only one sitting here with garlic breath."

"Thanks," he said, picking up a couple. "Garlic fries are weird."

"And yet you're eating them."

"I didn't say they didn't taste good."

"They also ward off vampires."

His gaze turned amused. "That's important."

I thought it all over, me and him and the world and everything. It actually didn't take long. Maybe I was tired. Or maybe I trusted him more than I realized. "The real reason I don't date is that I can't sleep with another person in the house. And eventually, sex and sleepovers generally tend to happen. It's all part of encouraging intimacy, right?"

He nodded.

"But I need to be able to get up and check the locks and make sure no one's in the yard, and change positions three hundred times and have the occasional nightmare without worrying if I'm disturbing someone else."

"Is this fact or theory?" he asked, not unkindly.

"Fact. When I first came back to town, I had a special male friend in Falls Creek. It didn't work out."

"Okay."

"The thing is, even asleep, other people make noises," I continued. "They snore or breathe loudly or turn this way and that and kick off the covers. Then, even if I've managed to get to sleep, I get startled and can't get back to sleep and it's all a big nightmare. I stand a much better chance of getting some shut-eye if it's just me in my space. Which means I'm not really open to developing an ongoing thing with another person."

"You mean like a relationship?"

"Yes. And it's not as if I just accept that I'm always going to have issues surrounding this stuff," I said, feeling the need to explain the whole sorry mess. "I've been pushing at some of my boundaries and I made that appointment, like I told you."

"It's okay," he said. "I'm not judging you. Thank you for telling me. Which boundaries have you been pushing, if you don't mind me asking?"

I hesitated. "I've never discussed any of this stuff with anyone besides Maria and Cézanne."

He just waited.

"I've been reading on my front porch after sunset. It might not sound like a big thing, but it's not something I've been ready to do before now," I said. "It always made me feel unsafe and exposed in the past. But I'm starting to work my way through that. The other thing I feel like I should tell you is that I can hear you some nights. Playing your guitar and singing and working on your new songs."

"You can hear me?"

"Yes. Through my bedroom window. And I know you moved out here for privacy, so . . ."

"No. That's okay. I don't mind you listening." He licked his lips. "But thanks for letting me know."

"Hey, Gary," said Josh from a nearby table.

Garrett tipped his chin.

"Nice to see you two sitting together getting along." And the wink Josh gave me was not subtle at all. Then he said, "No hard feelings about the other night at the town meeting, huh? Game of pool later?"

"Sounds good."

Josh did finger guns in reply.

I smiled. "Was there something you wanted to tell me?"

"Hmm?"

"You asked me to tell you something personal. Usually that means there's something on your mind that you want to tell me."

"Ah, yeah." His forehead furrowed. "I've started listening to the messages Grace left on my cell again. A while back, I made myself stop, but ever since ..."

"The mistake?" I asked quietly.

He sighed. "Yeah. There's this one message from when we were fighting. I can't even remember what the argument was about. But the names she called me. And she doesn't stop—it just goes on and on. Little fucking wonder I wasn't picking up the phone. But I can't stop listening to it. She was glorious when she was pissed off. And inventive as all hell."

I smiled.

"I'm not used to talking about her. But I hate this feeling lately like she's slipping away from me. Like I'm losing even the memory of her, you know?"

I just nodded.

"And that's all I've got left," he said, expression somber. "Memories."

"Have you considered grief counseling?"

He shrugged.

"Just an idea."

"I'm not exactly against it, just ... I don't know. Grace and I actually went to couples counseling a few times soon after we were married. To help us figure out how to communicate better. We had good times and bad, like any relationship. The industry can be hell on couples, and Grace found it hard to trust. She'd been let down so many times before," he said, his voice low.

His gaze stayed on his fingers, tapping out a beat against the tabletop. "It's why she didn't want to go out with me. Swore she was done with musicians. Said having a spoonful of talent didn't make up for us all being narcissistic pricks, coming in and swinging our dicks around. And she was right. I was a nightmare in my twenties. It took me a while to realize that just because everyone around me was saying the sun shone out of my ass didn't actually make it true. Selling *x* number of records or winning some award doesn't actually make you a good person."

"No?"

"No," he said. "We fought a lot, Grace and me, but we always made up. We'd only been married three years and together two before that. When you're both spending so much time on the road, that's not long. I thought we'd have more time."

An old slow song played on the jukebox.

He said no more. I didn't know what to say. While I'd been through some tough times, I'd never loved and lost like that. My heart hurt for him.

"Did I make things weird, telling you that?" he asked. "Talking about her?"

"No. Not at all. I'm just thinking deep thoughts. I don't want to say the wrong thing."

Now and then, it pays to be brave. Garrett was being brave talking about all of this with me. And all the while his fingers kept tapping. I reached out and covered his hand with my own. His skin was so warm against mine. For a moment, he just stared at our joined hands, with a blank face. And then I sat back with my hands in my lap, because we didn't need to be touching.

"So." I swallowed hard. "Would I have liked you in your twenties?"

"Not a chance. You can ask Smith—I was an asshat. Of course, so was he. You get successful and it's easy to get surrounded by certain types of people. Ones who have a vested interest in pacifying you and keeping you producing. The money is all that they care about. It also just does take some of us a little longer to grow up than others."

I smiled. "I bet you have some stories, though."

"You bet right." His smile was small, but it was there. "I've seen things that—"

"Ani?" said a horribly familiar voice.

And there, standing at the end of our booth, was my ex.

"Chad," I said, definitely not using a happy tone of voice. "I didn't know you were back."

"We need to talk."

My ex was a handsome white man with dark hair and blue eyes. So I had a type, apparently. Where he wildly differed from Garrett was in just about everything else. Chad's sense of entitlement and superiority complex were huge. It was partly my fault, since I'd put him on a pedestal. He'd been the designated town hot guy of my generation and when he wanted little old me . . . *oof*.

I was so grateful for his attention that I didn't even stop to think if he was worth all of the fuss. Our relationship was fine for the first year or so. For as long as I made him the center of my world. But then the thing happened and my priorities changed. Self-care was required. He didn't like that.

And if I didn't talk to him now, he would make a scene like a spoiled man-child. Guaranteed. Best to just get it over and done with.

"Excuse me, Garrett," I said. "This won't take long."

Before I could slide out of the booth, he was moving, giving up his seat. "I'll be around if you need me," was all he said, giving my ex a warning look.

Chad puffed himself up like a blowfish. "What the hell was that about?"

"What do we have to discuss?" I asked. "Why are you here?"

He scowled and took the seat opposite me. "Mom had a fall. I'm just back to check on her."

"I'm sorry. I didn't know. How is she?"

"Hairline fracture in the wrist. She'll be fine," he said in a dismissive tone of voice. "What's this about you being mayor?"

"Yeah." I shrugged. "Guess people wanted a change."

"But you're not doing it, right?"

I cocked my head. "Why wouldn't I?"

"Because you're not staying in Wildwood. I mean, why would you?" he asked. "You can't seriously be considering working in a general store for the rest of your life? There's nothing here for you. We both always agreed on that. C'mon, Ani. You've got to come back to L.A. eventually."

"No, I don't."

"Yes," he said as if correcting a child, "you do. Don't be ridiculous. I know you needed some time, but—"

"How's that nice girlfriend of yours?" I gave him my best fake smile. "The one with the crystal vagina eggs?"

He smirked. "See. You're jealous."

"Oh, trust me, I am so not even a little."

"It didn't work out." My smile might be fake, but his was the smarmiest in all the land. "This is what I'm saying. There's more for you in L.A. than you're thinking."

"I take it you mean you?" I asked. "Believe it or not, that is not a lure. Chad, we broke up four years ago. We are ancient history. Where is all this even coming from?"

"We used to have fun, didn't we? Maybe it's time for us to try again." He gave me a good slow, gratuitous looking over. Then he told my tits in their white halter-neck, "Christian was right, you're looking good. You kind of let yourself go for a while there. But now . . ."

"Chad, we're not together. Keep your eyes on my face and stop being a letch. And let me assure you, I have less than nil interest in your good buddy Christian's opinion of me."

He laughed. "Ani, calm down. We're just talking. Gosh. You always were emotional. I was paying you a compliment."

"Yeah. I really hadn't missed your gaslighting. It's time for you to leave."

"What? No. Honey—"

"Do not *honey* me."

"Hey now," he said in a pacifying tone of voice.

"Go away, Chad. We're done here."

"No one tells me what to do in my town." His expression turned ugly. "Look at you, dressing up for the fucking rock star. You're making a damn fool out of yourself and everyone knows. It's all they can talk about."

"So that's what you really think, huh?"

"I'm just trying to be honest with you."

"Go fuck yourself."

"There's no need to be like that," he gritted out. "I just wanted you to know what they're saying. I'm trying to help."

"Oh, please. Let me make this simple for you. We broke up four years ago. You have not spent the last four years pining for me, and I have absolutely no interest in spending quality time with you, now or ever."

"I know I didn't handle things as well as I could have after what happened."

I held up a hand. "No. Don't go there. It's not open for discussion."

"Look at you trying to get rid of me. That's not how you used to feel," he said. "You used to practically cling to me, you were so fucking scared someone would steal me away."

"Thank goodness I learned better." I slid my butt across the seat toward the exit. "Good night. Give your mother my best."

Whip fast, he reached out and grabbed my arm. "We're not done talking."

"Let go of me."

He leaned in closer. "Honey, you need to shut up and listen. I'm trying to help. I know what's best for you, if you'd just—"

A large hand grabbed hold of his wrist and squeezed. The sound that came out of Chad's mouth was startled, high, and full of pain. His fingers unlocked from around my arm. I immediately tucked it against my chest.

"Get out of the booth," said Garrett, not letting go.

Chad did as told, his face turning red with rage.

"Let's take a walk outside."

With a curse, Chad tore his wrist from Garrett's hold. His chin went up as he took in the audience. Because of course we had the attention of the whole bar. "Fine," he said, and stomped toward the door.

Garrett followed without a word. But his hands were curled tight into fists.

This could not be happening. One minute my night had been fine. There'd I'd been, hanging out in my favorite booth with one of my favorite people. Now this.

I followed close behind the two men. All of the bar's clientele poured out into the parking lot. It had been a while since Wildwood had seen a good throw-down. There'd been an outburst from some bored lumberjacks a few months back, resulting in the destruction of a couple of chairs. But Yong was not shy about banning people from the bar. And no one at the end of a long day wanted to have to drive all the way down to Falls Creek for a drink. Everyone knew they charged more for their craft beer.

"Don't do this," I said. "Please."

But too late. As soon as Chad cleared the steps and stood on the asphalt, he turned and swung at Garrett. His fist slammed into the side of his face, and Garrett's head snapped back at the impact. *Ouch.*

"Now that everyone's seen you attack me," said Garrett, cracking his neck, "guess I better defend myself."

And it was on.

My heart galloped inside my chest. "Someone stop them!"

"Stop them?" Josh laughed. "This is the most fun we've had in ages. I've got five dollars on Gary. Who's taking the bets?"

Fists were flying and blood was dripping, and I kind of wanted to vomit.

"Ooh," said Claude with a wince. "That had to hurt."

"Garrett will be fine, Ani. Take a look," said Yong, cradling a baseball bat. "Chad's slowing down already. He's gotten city soft."

Then Garrett smacked Chad in his stupid mouth and it was over. The whole thing had lasted a minute at most. In slow motion, Chad stumbled back a step before landing on his butt in the parking lot. And there he stayed.

"You don't come near her ever again. You don't talk to her, and you sure as hell don't touch her," said Garrett. And the fury on his face. Whoa. His nostrils were flaring and everything. "Do you understand?"

Chad said nothing. Just sat in the dust with blood dripping out of his nose in a steady stream. His good friend Christian, however, wandered in from out of the shadows and his eyes were wide with surprise. He helped Chad to his feet and dragged him to a waiting truck. Good riddance.

People started cheering and slapping Garret on the back. Because they were ridiculous. Obviously.

Josh looked at me and frowned. "But he won. Why are you upset?"

"Men are such idiots," said Emma with a wisdom born of the ages. Then she turned to Yong and said, "You better do something."

Yong looked between me and Garrett and nodded. "All right, everybody!" he yelled. "Time to get your asses back inside. Next round is on Garrett. Right, G?"

Garrett waved a hand as if to say "whatever."

It worked. Everyone rushed back inside. Then it was just me and him. Blood dripped from the knuckles on his right hand. Color surrounded one of his eyes and his cheek had already started to swell. Beneath a sky full of stars in the parking lot at the Wildwood Bar and Grill, the rock star gave me a wary glance. He was the epitome of beauty all disheveled. But I still wanted to throw something at him, just the same.

"I don't even know what to say," I admitted, walking down the steps to the asphalt. "How bad is your hand?"

"It'll be fine." Nice and slow, he flexed his fingers. "Before you say anything else, I couldn't just let him grab you. He was hurting you. I could see it in your face."

The music coming from inside was muffled by the wooden walls. Violence wasn't exactly unusual in Wildwood. But being the reason for it was shocking.

"There's no excuse for Chad's behavior," I said. "He was always a bit of a jerk, but he never used to be like that."

Garrett just grunted and watched me in silence.

The anger and anxiety in me finally bubbled to the surface. In all honesty, I didn't know what to do with it all. There was just too much emotion. "What if your hand had been broken? What if someone recorded the fight? Holy shit, Garrett, this could be an absolute disaster! You can't just—"

"I don't just go around picking fights like some fucking Neanderthal, and you know it." He towered over me with a cranky expression of his own. "But don't ask me to stand by and do nothing while some asshole hurts you. Because honest to fucking God, I can't do it, babe."

I froze.

"And it would kind of be unreasonable for you to ask me to. I mean think about it, if we got surrounded by fans and someone was trying to take a piece out of me for a souvenir, you would not be okay with that. You would try to stop them." He paused and pondered for a moment. "Guess you wouldn't invite them out to a parking lot for a fistfight. But you get my point."

Yeah. I still had nothing.

He raised his hand to his ribs and winced. "What I'm saying is, my behavior tonight might have been a little extreme, but it wasn't totally implausible. And if the media gets wind of it or he presses charges, I'll handle it. I'll protect you. Okay?"

I kept right on giving him my best impression of a deer caught in headlights.

"Why do I keep feeling the need to explain myself to you? Are you going to say something?" he asked eventually. "Ani?"

"You, um, you called me 'babe.'"

He blinked. "I did?"

"Yeah."

Nothing from him.

"It's not a big deal," I added. "It's probably something you do with various females occasionally without thinking, right?"

The first sign that something was wrong was the little line appearing between his brows. Like there might be a problem here, but he wasn't quite sure. This, however, was soon followed by an expression of shock. And holy heck, hadn't we just been through all of this recently?

"A friendly thing, yeah?" I took a deep breath, flipped my hair back, and forged ahead. "I thought as much. I just hadn't realized you did that and it caught me by surprise. But no big deal. We should go inside and get some ice on your hand. That would be the smart thing to do."

The man didn't move a muscle, and the look in his eyes could best be described as existential dread. As if he'd put his soul to the test and it had come back wanting. Not good.

"Garrett? It's okay. Really."

Shoulders slumped, he stared at some point past my shoulder. Gazing into his past, most likely. He was gone beyond where I could reach him, and it hurt. I should have kept my mouth shut. Ignored the endearment. But no. Because I was an idiot.

My eyes were itching and it was time to go. "I'm going to go inside and give you a minute."

For someone who said she didn't want to be in a relationship, I sure had a bad habit of getting myself into fixes with this man.

"I don't call other women 'babe,'" he said.

I stopped and turned on the first step. "Oh."

"It's not a nickname I give friends." His Adam's apple bobbed in his thick throat. "And I didn't call Grace that, either. I wasn't mistaking you for her, so don't think that."

Then he looked at me, and I looked at him, and ugh. This situation. The amount of things between us. Both real and imagined and everything in between. But if one of us was going to make a move, it had to be him. Because he'd called kissing me a mistake, and I wasn't wearing the blame if it happened again.

At long last, he took a step forward, then another and another. The last one delivered him to the bottom of the stairs, standing right in front of me. But still the inches felt like miles. We were the same height this way. I could look him straight in the eyes and see it all. While a hint of fear lingered, there were other emotions too. Things like lust and longing. And those I understood all too well.

I licked my lips. "Are you going to say something?"

"No, babe," he said, and leaned in and kissed me.

Chapter Eleven

ARRETT OPENED THE DOOR TO HIS HOUSE AT EIGHT o'clock the following night. He had offered to walk me over, but I could cover the distance from my house to my neighbor's on my own in the dark. And Gene was out in the yard following the fence line, giving me doggy smiles the whole way. It was fine. The idea of actually going on a date with the rock star, however, was messing with my head.

He was wearing black jeans and a matching tee. No shoes. Honest to God, the man was giving me a foot fetish. And who didn't prefer to be barefoot at home? Half of his dark hair was tied back in a man bun and the overall look was just one of casual, comfortable yum. The black eye he was sporting gave him an interesting edge of rough.

Meanwhile, I was wearing a strapless embroidered midi dress in pale blue with beige sandals and matching clutch, with my hair up in a crown of braids. Cézanne and I had discussed it all at great length this morning and it had seemed a fun outfit at the time. A little bit romantic and fancy, but fun. In comparison to him, however, it just seemed extreme.

And then there was the way his eyes went wide at the sight of me.

"I'm overdressed," I said, taking a step back. "This is just a casual thing and I . . . Let me go change real quick. I'll put on some jeans and be right back."

"Please don't."

I hesitated.

"You look beautiful. I've never seen you in a dress before." His smile was small, but very much present. "Stay. You're fine. Fuck. You're much more than fine."

And still I hesitated. Dating was even more nerve-wracking than I remembered.

He held out his hand to me and I took it, and yeah. Okay. Much better. I don't think we'd ever held hands properly before. But the warmth of his skin and the way his fingers wrapped me up made everything perfect. Maybe we could do this after all.

"Come on," he said, leading the way.

Gene nudged us aside and went to check on his food bowl. Because priorities.

"So . . . dating, huh?" I smiled. "I haven't done this in four years."

"I haven't done this in seven years."

"You win."

It must be discombobulating. To think that you've found the one and you're married and done with the whole dating scene, only to find yourself back there. But he'd asked me to dinner after kissing me the night before and so, here we were. It had been surreal, walking back into the bar together after the fight.. People sure gave us a lot of knowing looks. Then Garrett had the good mind to buy everyone in the bar another round of drinks. It distracted them just fine.

All while I tried to figure out what I was more afraid of— Garrett and me actually getting together, or him yet again changing his mind. Hard to say.

Back to the here and now: The house had been meticulously cleaned. The man had been busy. None of the chaos and carnage from the days after Grace's birthday remained. Florence + the Machine played on the record player and mood lighting was the go.

But we didn't stop there. He led me on into the kitchen, where the table was set and pillar candles were lit. A crystal vase of white roses sat at one end of the table, along with a bottle of wine in a bucket of ice. And dinner was served and waiting. Steak and lobster with dinner rolls, a garden salad, onion rings, and fries.

I didn't know what to say. No one had ever done anything like this for me.

"Wow," I said at last.

"Don't be too impressed. I had a restaurant in Eureka do it. Claude told me what you'd like. A florist sent up the candles and bouquet." He gripped the back of his neck and . . . oh my God. Was he actually blushing? "You do like steak and lobster, right?"

"I would have been happy with ramen. But this is amazing."

He gave me side-eye. "You would not have been happy with ramen."

"Eh. I might have thought you were a little slack. But in the end I wouldn't have cared."

"Come on, sit," he said, pulling out a chair.

I did as told, placing the white linen napkin on my lap. "We're really doing this."

"Yes." He sat opposite and poured the white wine. "How are you dealing with that?"

"Quietly terrified."

"Me too."

"You used to date supermodels—what have you got to be worried about?" I joked. Then I shut my mouth and hung my head. "Can we pretend I didn't say that?"

"It's fine."

"My hobbies include blurting out silly inconsiderate shit when I'm nervous. And you make me nervous like . . . all the time."

"We're both going to get through this," he said. "It's what I've been telling myself for the last twenty-four hours."

"No regrets?" I asked. "Because, I mean, if you've changed your mind, I would under—"

"I haven't changed my mind. But let's just take it slow and see what happens, yeah?"

"Slow is great. I am . . . yes, I'm very into slow." I nodded and carefully started dissecting dinner. Which was when Gene nudged my elbow with a wet doggy nose.

"Don't fall for it," said Garrett. "He's already had his share."

"Nice try, puppy. But no."

With a hearty sigh, Gene flopped to the floor. Never had a dog been so maligned.

Then Garrett said, "I know you're sitting over there waiting for me to freak out again, but it's not going to happen."

"How do you know that? Just out of interest. Because you

were pretty much ready to spend the rest of your days ignoring me after that first kiss."

"I *am* sorry about that. But I'm not in denial about us anymore."

"What changed?"

"Last night, when you said I'd called you 'babe,' you were being nice about it and giving me an out. At the time. But once you'd had a chance to think about it, you would have been hurt and angry. And you would have had every right to be. You were already trying to protect yourself and keep your distance. If I tried to distance *myself* from calling you babe, it wouldn't have been good," he said, tone serious. "I couldn't keep playing with your heart."

I just nodded.

"So here we are." Garrett took a sip of wine, watching me all the while with knowing eyes. It was the difference between him and other men. He knew how to love. But he also knew how painful it was to have his heart broken. "This isn't a mistake, Ani. I don't know what the hell it is. But it's not a mistake."

"Okay."

He winced and shook his head. "That's a lie. The whole not-denying thing is going to take some practice. But I *do* know what this is. It's just a big deal admitting it, you know?"

"Yeah."

It was us trying to be something. Together. But we didn't need to say it out loud. Here we were on our first real live date. Actions spoke louder than words.

"And as I recall, you repeatedly and emphatically said you did not want to date," he said. "How's that working out for you?"

"We're turning the truth levels right up to awkward, huh?" I asked.

"Babe, when haven't we?"

"Good point."

"Tell me what you're thinking."

I set down my silverware. "Well . . . I'm sitting here wearing the fanciest dress I own, wondering if you're going to take it off me later."

"I've been wondering about that too." The candlelight flickered, reflected in his calm gaze. At least one of us had their shit together. "On that front, it's been a little over two years for me."

"Just under four for me."

"You win that one."

"Great." I laughed. "As for how I feel about being here on a date with you . . ."

"Besides being nervous. Which is going around."

"Right." I took a deep breath and let it out slowly. Anything to stop my heart from spontaneously combusting. "I have a hard time saying no to you. I don't like staying away from you. In the short amount of time I've known you, you've become very important to me. That being said, my issues regarding dating as we've previously discussed are still of concern."

He nodded slowly. "Okay."

"And then there's the whole thing where it's a little hard to believe that I'm sitting here with you sometimes. The end." I picked my silverware back up and got to eating. Because the food was delicious and amazing and deserved my attention. Though my stomach was doing a lot of tipping and turning.

After a few minutes of silence, however, I asked, "How about you?"

He picked up an onion ring, examined it, and set it back down. "This is happening sooner than I anticipated. I figured I'd probably meet someone eventually, you know? Just not so soon. Two years is a while, I guess, but . . . I don't know."

"You still feel guilty about me?"

"Sometimes," he admitted.

I sat in silence.

"I'm not always sure what to do, because the grief is still there. It's confusing. Trying to figure out what the fuck I'm feeling," he said. "But since the first time we talked, it's like you've taken up residence in this corner of my mind."

"Please. You did not like me the first time we met."

"What I didn't like was my reaction to you."

I took another sip of wine. It was good. Almost good enough to make me not mind how easily this man kept stealing pieces of my heart. "Enough deep and meaningful. Let's give this beautiful meal the attention it deserves and make light and easy conversation. I insist."

"Okay," he said, cutting into his steak. "Talk to me. Tell me about your day, your friends, family, work, what you've been reading or watching on TV, or whatever. I want to hear about it all."

"You do, huh?"

Given he was chewing on his food, he just nodded.

I owed a debt of gratitude to my junior drama club for helping me to keep a straight face. Though the mini heart attack his words caused, I couldn't do much about. Guarding my emotions against him was getting harder by the moment. He wanted to know about me. All about me. That had happened before approximately never. Which really made me wonder what I'd been doing dating all of those losers in my younger years.

I pasted on a smile. "Okay, Garrett. Whatever you want."

"It's chocolate bourbon pecan torte," said Garrett in the light from a dozen candles and the fridge. The way the light lit the planes of his face. How it made shadows of his cheekbones and the cut of his jaw. He was a work of art. "What do you think?

"Maybe later."

He shut the fridge door. "You got it. What's up next? What do people even do on dates these days?"

"Um. We could dance."

"I don't really dance."

"You're a musician," I said. "What the heck do you mean, you don't dance?"

He ruffled up his hair. A totally boyish and charming move. "I'm not actually that good at it, to be honest."

"Ugh."

"That's a deal breaker, huh?"

"I guess it's not the end of the world."

"The way you say it kind of sounds like it might be," he said, almost smiling.

"I'm disappointed. What can I say?"

"Was really hoping you wouldn't feel that way at least until the morning after."

"It's good to have dreams, Garrett."

He bit back a smile. Totally got him that time.

"Let me think, what else can we do? Hmm." I tried to think big thoughts, but it didn't work. Being here with him felt good and right. Much more than was safe or slow. Something had to be done about this, for both our sakes. "You know, you've never shown me upstairs."

"You want to see upstairs?"

"Yeah." And I gave him a smile before kicking off my shoes and turning and running for the stairs. Because who the fuck wouldn't want to see a turret?

"Shit. Babe. Be careful."

I was puffing by the time I made it to the top of the staircase and clutching my skirt in my hand. However, I had successfully infiltrated Garrett's private zone. Which was kind of like the danger zone, but not quite. To the left was another set of stairs going up to the attic. Straight ahead were three guest bedrooms. To the right was the main bedroom, and oh yeah. This I had to see, because I was nosy as fuck when it came to him.

The walls were painted a dark charcoal, and the bed was this massive and mighty thing with four posts all painted black. In all honesty, it made my panties damp. Just the thought of him sleeping there. Alone. Though looking at him by candlelight for the last hour or two had left me a hormonal and heartsore mess. This had to be how fairy-tale princesses felt. High on life and loving it all. Trying to figure out their Prince Charming and what came next. And what came next for us was going to be damn good.

Garrett leaned against the door frame, watching me with interest. "What do you think?"

I turned a slow circle, taking it all in. The huge windows looking out to the woods and river beyond. High ceilings and crisp white linen on the bed. Smooth, polished wooden floor beneath my feet and the way it all smelled faintly of him.

Sex between us could definitely be used to slow things down. I was a certified genius. There was no way a healthy, virile man like Garrett would rather keep having deep and meaningful conversations with me when we could be banging.

Protect the heart by sacrificing the loins. It was a yes from me. He could make me date him apparently, but he couldn't keep making me show him my soul and tell him all of my secrets.

"I like it," I said with a sexy smile.

"Knocked out the wall to the next bedroom to put in the en suite and walk-in wardrobe. It's not like I need more than three guest bedrooms."

"You have a chandelier in your bedroom."

"It's vintage. Grace was into things like that."

I smiled gently. "She had great taste."

He nodded.

"In a lot of things."

He snorted. "Thanks."

"New bed?"

"Ah, yeah. Yes. It is."

"Okay. Good to know." I wandered toward the en suite. "It's all very luxury and mood lighting, Garrett."

"You want me to turn up the light?"

"Hell no."

A big old claw-foot tub dominated the space in the bathroom. Accompanied by a massive walk-in shower and gray quartz countertops. All of it complemented by those views of the local area that seemed to go on forever. It suited him, the play of shadows and light. The old Cooper house had never looked so fine; I think the old lady would have approved. A whole new life for the place. And a whole new life for him—if that's what he wanted.

"You're in a strange mood," he said, from closer than before.

"Am I?"

"Yeah. I can't track you at all."

"Track me?" I asked with a smile.

"You know what I mean."

"I know what you mean."

The man was standing in the en suite doorway, watching me. I couldn't read him any better than he could me. That was the truth. But he was getting seduced tonight whether he liked it or not.

I moved closer and rested my hand lightly on his chest. "What are you thinking?"

"I, ah . . ." His gaze roved over me, taking in my face and my body. And the longing in his eyes wasn't just my imagination. We were both in up to our necks with these emotions. "I don't know. My mind's a mess."

"What do you want, Garrett?"

"When it comes to you?" he asked. "A hell of a lot. But first, tell me . . . Why'd you run straight for my bedroom?"

"Because I'm nosy."

"And?"

"And I want to get into your pants. I thought that was obvious."

He raised his brows. "We're just going straight there, huh?"

"Why not?" I upped my sexy smile to a coquettish grin. It had been a while. But I'm pretty sure it still worked. I presented him with the back of my dress. "Can you help me with the zipper?"

His intake of breath was audible. "Shit."

"I've been thinking about it, and I think we should just go for it. Just do it."

"Is that so?"

"Or I can go home. Or we can go back downstairs." I watched him process it all over my shoulder. Some eyelash fluttering may have been involved. "It's your choice. But you know what I want. What I *really* want."

He cocked his head. "To avoid actual intimacy by fucking?"

"What?" I screeched. "No. I . . . that's not what I'm doing."

"Babe," he said in a chiding tone. "First you're adamant that you don't want to date. But here you are on a date with me. Then at dinner you're very definite about agreeing to take it slow and want to talk about light and easy things. Now you're giving me fuck-me eyes and asking me to take off your dress. What does it look like to you?"

"So you don't want to have sex with me?"

"Oh, I want inside you like you wouldn't believe. But if you think trying to make things purely physical between us is going to work, you're kidding yourself."

"We could try."

"If you like," he said, nonplussed. "But I'm warning you now, if we have sex, we're cuddling after."

I groaned. "Are you serious?"

"Absolutely. I'm not putting out otherwise."

I tipped my head back and looked at the ceiling. "Fine. Whatever. Undo the dress."

"I wasn't expecting you," he said in a more contemplative tone of voice.

"No," I agreed. "I wasn't expecting you, either. I was going to quite happily live out my life next door with the addition of a dog and cat, maybe. But with a town and a job and people that I love. Just a whole lot of peace, you know?"

He nodded.

"But here we are, making things complicated."

"Yeah," he agreed.

I waited, my heart in my throat.

He stepped closer, and the warmth of his breath on the back of my neck was sublime. His hands slid over my shoulders, fingers caressing my neck. And oh, he could touch me forever and a day. The feel of his skin on mine.

"The things I want to do to you," he said softly.

"Oh?"

"This is . . . it's important to me, okay?"

"I know," I admitted. "Me too."

And ever so slowly, he pulled the zipper on the dress down the length of my back. Not stopping until it draped loosely around me. The pads of his fingers traced my spine, pushing the bunched-up fabric over my hips and down to the floor. Going, going, gone. His firm grip on my hips was everything. Like my world began and ended right here and now with him. This moment had it all.

With his face buried in my neck and the press of him against my back. I held his head to me, threading my fingers through his hair. We just stood there leaning against each other for the longest moment. The intimacy of it got to me. Being in his room with him late at night, all alone. It was beautiful and full of meaning, no matter how much I might try to deny same.

Gentle fingers trailed over the scar high on the side of my neck that I usually tried to keep hidden. Hair or makeup usually did the trick. He traced its path up behind my ear. But he didn't ask me about it. Thank goodness.

"Stay with me," he said out of nowhere.

"I'm not going anywhere."

"Thank you." He ground his burgeoning hard-on against my ass. "Before I lose my head, where are we at with safety?"

"Do you have condoms?"

"Shit. No. I didn't think."

"Me neither. It's been so long. I was so worried about everything else that I forgot about that."

"Yeah."

"I'm negative. I, um, it's not the right time of the month," I said. "But you should know I'm not on any birth control."

His teeth imprinted on my shoulder ever not so gently. "I'm negative too. Not the right time of the month?"

"No."

My strapless bra loosened before Garrett tossed it aside. "Fuck. Babe."

And I happy sighed, because bras really are the worst fucking thing ever. But Garrett's big hands were divine. He cupped my breasts and I was kind of in heaven. The way his thumbs played over my nipples. Just knowing it was him touching me. Only the feel of his lips sliding across the side of my neck could beat it. Talk about happiness. "I feel like my vagina would mount an insurrection if we stopped now. We could do other things, though, if you're more comfortable with that?"

"This is us, right?"

"What?"

"This is us," he repeated. "This is you and me now. We're seeing this through."

"Yeah," I agreed with a sigh of defeat. "It's you and me now."

"Thank fuck."

His hands spun me and then we were face-to-face. Hell yes. Nothing could beat his lips on mine, his tongue in my mouth. The sheer heat and power of him. When Garrett finally let himself go, it was all gracious and good.

My hands shoved his tee up and over and off. His skin was hotter and better pressed against my bare breasts. Any other time I'd been to bed with someone, it had been play in comparison. It had been convenient or pleasant or I don't know what. But not important like this. Trying to make it purely physical between us was already a complete and utter failure.

Then he went to get to his knees, and no. Oh no. His fingers tangled in my panties and he was already tugging them down my legs.

"Wait."

"What?" he asked, lips already damp and swollen from kissing. "What's wrong?"

"I just had a thought. I think it would be best if you stayed where I can see you."

He cocked his head. "You don't want me to give you head?"

"While in theory that sounds like the best idea ever, I want you to stay nice and close where I can keep an eye on you. Just in case."

He placed an open-mouthed kiss against my cunt. Talk about unfair. Because the man knew how to use his tongue. And it was such a long, strong, and talented muscle. Little wonder he was a singer. The way his fingers dug into my hips and how he looked on his knees. The tip of his tongue flicking back and forth over my clit and oh God. It was a lot.

My insides tensed and my blood ran hot and nothing had ever been this good. Nothing ever could.

"You're wet," he said, voice guttural. "I fucking love that. And you smell so good."

I grabbed a handful of his hair for good luck. "Oh, God. Garrett."

"Hmm?"

"I mean it. Come up here." I tugged on his hair. "If you accidentally freak out, then I need to see the moment it happens so we deal with it together."

With a sigh, he got to his feet and wiped his face with the palm of his hand. "Fine."

"Thank you."

"Though I think you're being overly cautious."

"Let's agree to disagree."

I didn't mean to get cock-struck with the imprint of his hard-on pressing against the front his black jeans. But it was there, and whoa.

"Yeah," he said, grabbing my hand and leading me toward the bed. "In the middle of the mattress with your legs spread. Please. If I can't lick, I can at least look."

Given it wasn't a totally ridiculous request, I acquiesced with reasonable grace. At least, I thought so.

"That's not spread." He undid the button and zipper on his jeans and shoved them down, taking his black boxer briefs with him. The long, thick length of his cock pointed to the ceiling, and okay. This was really happening. It would be easy to get addicted to the way his gaze heated with such lust. "Now you decide to get shy?"

"What?"

Naked and beautiful, he climbed onto the bed. His big body parting my legs wide and making himself right at home in the cradle of my thighs. "Better," he said, taking my mouth with his. Kissing Garrett made my head spin in dizzy circles. Actual sex with the man might just end me.

"We're still taking it slowly, right?" I asked. Because my emotions needed to calm the hell down.

And he actually laughed. I didn't even know he could make such a sound. First one hand and then the other, he pressed my hands against the solid wood of the headboard. But with his tongue in my mouth, I found it hard to care what was happening. We were a hot, wet mess. The length of his cock slid back and forth through the lips of my sex and electricity was already racing up my spine. My legs wrapped around his hips, holding him to me. Given how good he felt, I might never let him go.

The blue of his eyes had never seemed so intense. His jaw was set and his focus wholly on me as he lined up the wide, blunt head of his cock with my entrance. Slow and steady, he pushed inside. And the sound he made. A groan that seemed to be drawn up from the very depths of his soul.

"You feel . . . fuck. Are we good?" he asked, the muscles in his arms quivering with how he was holding himself back. "Ani?"

"Yes." I nodded. "I've got you."

We stared at each other and he sank in deep. Not stopping until his hips rested against mine. The slick of sweat on his skin and we'd barely begun. I tightened on him, getting comfortable with his girth, and he hissed.

"Sorry," I said with a grin.

"You're fine. It's just been a while. Not sure how long I'll last."

"We've got all night." I smiled, my hand curled around the back of his neck. "No need to hold back, Garrett."

"I wanted to make love to you. But the way you feel . . ."

"It's okay. You can make love to me later."

"Are you sure?"

I nodded. "Yes."

With a feral grin, he pulled back and pushed in, faster and harder each time. More and more. Over and over. I braced myself against the headboard as he fucked into me. As he pushed my body up the mattress with the force of his thrusts. And he did all this while gazing into my eyes the whole time.

Sex had never meant this much. Like being with him, having him fill me up, made for a spiritual connection. Like he saw all of the parts of me I would never dare to reveal. We were one tangled mess of emotions and body parts and life histories, and it was all beyond good.

With a hand beneath my butt cheek, he angled my hips higher and started stroking against my clit with the base of his cock on every pass. My back arched and my hard nipples rubbed against his chest and . . . *fuck*. The way he filled me. How the friction made the sensation build like a hot knot of tension between my hips. His nostrils flared and his lips thinned and he fucked me like a man possessed. And he didn't look away for even a moment, keeping the bond between us.

My orgasm crept up on me. I came hard, breath hitched and heart beating out of time. My arms tightened around his neck, holding him to me.

With a growl, he shoved his cock in deep and came, hips pumping. There was just the warm scent of his skin and the smell of sex in the air. My whole happy world coalesced to this bed and this man. The long, heavy length of his body settled on top of me, and yes. I'd never been so delighted to be squished into a mattress. Never.

"You okay?" he asked eventually. His breath tickled my ear.

"Yeah. How about you?"

"I, um . . . yeah." He studied my face, searching for something. "You can stay, right?"

"I can stay."

"Did it work? Are your feelings safe from me now?"

"No," I admitted.

He sighed in relief. "Good. That's good."

Chapter Twelve

BEING IN ANOTHER HOUSE IN THE SMALL HOURS OF THE night was strange. The last time I'd tried this, it had been a dismal failure. But it wouldn't hurt to try again.

Garrett had said I could go wherever I wanted and do whatever I wanted. To make myself at home. I took him at his word. And if I decided to go to my actual home, he would walk me. He'd made me promise to wake him and not go it alone. But before crashing out on the bed, he showed me the security system, the positioning of surveillance cameras and smart alarms. The upstairs bathroom even doubled as a saferoom. It must have cost a fortune. And right now, every door and window leading to the outside was locked up tight. Theoretically, I couldn't be safer.

Gene followed me around the rooms on the ground level. I drifted from the parlor to the kitchen to the dining room, and then the sitting room. With my hair disheveled and wearing one of Garrett's button-down shirts, I must have looked like a ghost, wandering about in the dark. The whole world was shadows in the ambient light and I was part interloper/part explorer. I couldn't sleep because my brain was busy and my normal routine disrupted. But tonight there was the added bonus of another worry. That of Garrett's dead wife.

The fact that Grace had never actually been here in this house helped me relax a little. Her ideas and style were here. But she'd run out of time and never gotten to step foot inside the place. Maybe it made me cruel, being grateful for that fact. Though I think setting some boundaries with the dead wouldn't hurt. I was sleeping with her husband and walking through her house. However, her ownership of these things was in the past.

While it wasn't her choice to leave, she was gone. She would always have a part of Garrett's heart. It was a fact. And if I couldn't make peace with it, then I might as well leave. But there was room for me here. There had to be. I refused to be somebody's consolation prize. And being an insecure mess all of my days over my place in his heart wouldn't work. But the love we'd made in his bed upstairs was important and right and . . . I don't know.

Gene didn't like the stairs. I went back up alone, taking my clutch with me. And there was Garrett, sprawled out on the bed like a marble statue, all hard lines with breathtaking dips and valleys. He lay asleep on his back, wearing only a pair of boxer briefs. A dark smudge sat on his ribs from the fight, another covering his right eye. The moonlight loved him. My feelings were a touch more complicated but no less intense.

He wanted me here. It was enough for now.

The bedroom, with its huge black four-poster bed, charcoal walls, fireplace, and small sitting area—it was all very rock star. I made myself comfortable in a large wingback chair and stared at him and thought deep thoughts. Like how there was no way I was going home even if I didn't sleep a wink. I would happily sit there staring at him until dawn and count the hours not wasted.

And that's what I did until I finally fell asleep.

"Good morning, people," bellowed the large male standing in the bedroom doorway.

Jolted awake in this fashion, I went straight into fight-or-flight mode. I threw off the blanket someone had place on my lap and hit the floor on my knees. My breath heaved in and out of me in ragged gasps. What I needed was either a weapon or a place to hide. What I found was my beige clutch with a can of mace inside.

"Ani. Hey," said Garrett, grabbing me by the shoulders.

With my heartbeat hammering loud behind my ears, I couldn't hear a thing. In just another second, I would have realized. I would have recognized him. But barely awake and panicking under the weight of old trauma, all I knew was that strong hands had grabbed hold of me.

And that's how Garrett came to receive a face full of pepper spray. On the morning after our first night together. #fml

"I'm so sorry," I said.

Garrett sat at the dining table with a bowl full of cool saltwater. The internet said it was the best thing for dealing with capsicum spray. He rinsed out his eyes again, swearing all the while. "Not your fault."

"I bought you doughnuts from Earl's. I thought you'd be happy to see me." Smith leaned against the kitchen door frame and hung his blond head in shame. "And I would have thought landing a helicopter in your backyard would have woken everyone up."

"It did wake me up," said Garrett. "I was getting dressed. But I was letting her catch up on sleep."

"You landed a helicopter in the backyard?" I asked in amazement.

"Yeah. And we did accidentally trim a couple of the trees. Sorry about that." Smith grimaced. "Anyway, it's gone now. I sent it back."

"You shouldn't have. You're not staying," growled Garrett, still washing out his poor inflamed eyes.

"Sure I am," said Smith, unperturbed. "But we can talk about that later. Ani, you know I love you, but is your first reaction always to reach for the mace?"

"I, ah—"

"Don't answer that." Garrett blindly groped for a fresh cloth. "It's none of his fucking business."

"It's okay." If I just kept taking deep, even breaths, my lungs had to calm the fuck down eventually. "I have to talk about it sometime. And right now, I'm so horrified and embarrassed that it's actually kind of hard to feel anything else. But I do feel like I owe you both an explanation."

"You don't owe him or anyone else shit," said Garrett.

"He's right." Smith gave me a gentle smile. "But I'm here and I'm your friend. It's up to you if I take Gene out back for a walk or not. I'm fine with whatever you decide, babe."

"Do *not* call her 'babe,'" said Garrett.

Smith gave me a knowing smile. *Jerk.*

I thought it over. "Um. Yeah. Maybe if you could give us a minute, that would be best."

Smith nodded and called for the dog.

When the door to the back porch shut, I sighed loud and proud. "I'm so—"

"Don't say you're sorry again. It was an accident. And you didn't ruin anything."

"To the contrary, I made our first morning together truly memorable. You are never going to forget this."

Garrett finished patting his eyes dry and looked at me. Or tried to look at me. Despite washing them out for the last fifteen minutes, they were still red and swollen. "If now isn't the right time to talk about this stuff, I understand."

"I know." I wrapped my arms around myself good and tight. "I think I need to get it out, though. If I just say it quickly, I won't have to think about it too hard. Because carrying it around and keeping it secret is just making it bigger and heavier, okay?"

He nodded, gaze concerned.

"I was sleeping. A man broke into the apartment I shared with a friend. I woke up with him standing beside my bed, holding a knife to my neck, and I . . ." I swallowed past the tightness in my throat. "He had his hand over my mouth and he was so big and I was so scared. Just fucking terrified. I could barely even figure out what was going on. To wake up and have this stranger . . ."

Garrett sat perfectly still. I'm not even sure he was breathing.

I rubbed away a tear with the heel of my hand. Like I hadn't cried my heart out a hundred times over the years. It was a fine stress release, but I could do without the added drama just now. "I mean, I'm lucky, really. My friend came home with company.

She'd been out on a date. I must have made some noise, and they came to my bedroom door to check on me. The guy got spooked and ran. I survived with just the scar on my neck that you noticed last night. And a whole bundle of neuroses.

"I kind of fell apart after that. I didn't feel safe in the apartment, but I didn't want to go out, either. Living with that kind of fear hanging over you all the time, it . . . it's awful." I took a deep breath and calmed myself. "Coming home to Wildwood made the most sense. I could control my surroundings a bit better than I could in the city. Most of the faces were familiar to me, and my family and friends were here. Things didn't seem to set me off as often. It was just easier all around."

He nodded. "You slept here last night."

"Yeah. I, um, I fell asleep in the chair. I was watching you, actually."

His smile was gentle.

"Are you saying I was a big, brave girl for staying at my boyfriend's overnight?"

"Don't belittle it," he said. "It's not something you were able to do a few years ago."

"True."

For a moment, he just stared at me. With his blank face in place, it was impossible to tell how he was feeling. "You just called me your boyfriend."

"Yeah, ah . . . whatever. We don't have to put labels on things at this stage."

The corner of his mouth edged up a little. "Got to admit, mace is a new one, first-date wise," he said. "But I'm sorry to say it doesn't beat the time a Hollywood actress drove her Maserati into me and my hedge."

"She hit you and your garden with her expensive car?"

"She only bruised me. That section of the hedge was destroyed, though. It was an accident. She was reversing out of a tight spot and wasn't used to the vehicle," he said. "We were probably lucky that's the worst thing that happened."

"Huh."

"Was there anything else you wanted to tell me?"

I shook my head emphatically.

"Can I touch you now?" he asked.

I nodded. And that's how I found myself wrapped up in his arms. No place could be better. I pressed my face against his chest and listened to his steady heartbeat. Everything was okay. Everything was going to be fine.

Smith rushed back into the kitchen with a barking Gene hot on his heels, all het up. "Come on now. Good dog."

"What set him off?" asked Garrett with a frown.

Smith closed the door. "Sorry to be the bearer of bad news, man. But you've got lurkers up the top of the driveway. Looks like media with a long-range camera and a dozen or so fans. Lucky you put the big fence and gate in, huh?"

"Landing a chopper in my backyard was hardly subtle," growled Garrett.

"How are you going to get rid of them?" I asked with dawning horror.

"It's okay," said Garrett. "I'll sort it out. We knew this was going to happen sooner or later."

"Yeah, but . . . shit. I am not doing the walk of shame in front of paparazzi and your fans, Garrett. That is not happening."

Smith bit back a smile.

"This isn't funny," I said sharply.

"I know, I know." He held up his hands in surrender. "I'm just so happy to see you two getting along."

"You're not staying," repeated Garrett.

"Oh, relax, man. I'm the least of your problems right now."

Sadly for all of us, he was right.

Garrett the neighbor might now be mine. But Garrett the rock star remained an unknown quantity. This became obvious when he picked up his cell and started making calls.

Smith sat opposite me at the table, eating a doughnut and sipping coffee. "I love it when he goes all diva."

"Do you?"

The gentle giant just smiled.

"This is the strangest way to spend a Sunday."

"Hang in there, babe," he said.

"I heard that," said Garrett, giving his friend a death glare.

Smith kept on smiling. "Ani, if they don't know about you now, they will soon. Be ready. They'll have people sniffing around asking all sorts of questions. And someone will talk. Someone always talks."

I nodded.

"You lock down your social media?"

"Yeah."

"That's good. They're going to say all sorts of shit. But remember, none of them actually know you. Their job is to turn you into clickbait to make a buck or two. Nothing more and nothing less."

Garrett put down his cell, leaning his jeans-clad ass against the edge of the kitchen counter. "Stop scaring her."

"I'm not scaring her. I'm telling her the truth," said Smith in the same calm voice. "You want to keep her, you better prepare her for the shit storm that's about to hit. She's not like the girls you used to date down in L.A., man. If they weren't actually part of the industry, they were living on its edges. They knew. She doesn't."

I frowned. "I'm not an idiot."

"I never said that, darling." Smith took a sip of coffee. "The fact that you're not part of all that is a good thing. Believe me. But you still need to know what's coming at you."

"Don't call her 'darling,' either," said Garrett. "Just use her name."

"What are they going to say?" I asked.

Smith shrugged. "Lots of things. They might say you're his rebound. That you're only after him for his fame and money. And of course, they'll point out that you're the opposite of Grace."

"Am I really, though?"

Neither male said anything.

"I mean, I get that she was a svelte and statuesque redhead who was rich and famous. An award-winning singer/songwriter with a designer wardrobe who traveled the world on her private jet. Who attended all of the top parties and lived in a mansion in the Hollywood Hills." I paused. "Yeah. Okay. I think I just answered my own question. We're complete and total opposites."

Smith gave Garrett a pointed look.

Garrett sighed. "You're two different people. And you're different from each other in lots of ways. Grace always had to be doing something. She had all of this energy all of the time and always had a dozen projects on the go. Work and other stuff, like this house. It could be hard, trying to keep up with her. And she was a perfectionist, which could get damn old. Her parents pushed her, raised her to be a real overachiever. Started her out in the business early and everything."

"Okay," I said. "In comparison, I sound like a small-town, lazy loser."

"Your ability to chill and compromise occasionally is not a bad thing." Smith tied back his long blond hair. "Trust me. And I happen to like your small town, Mayor Bennet. What I've seen of it so far."

"You're not staying," said Garrett. "We should have some help and supplies in an hour or two."

"Right. I've been thinking I could call my cousin, Astrid, and ask her to bring me some of her clothes since we're a similar size," I said. "And I can go crash at her place. She has a solid fence around her yard. The sheriff always liked her, too; he'll clear any lurkers out in no time. Because if I leave here and go straight next door to my house, they're just going to follow me, right?"

"Most likely." The little line appeared between his brows. "You want to leave?"

"You want me to stay?"

"Babe, I *am* the reason you're in this mess."

My heart skipped a beat. "I know you feel responsible for this situation. But as you said before, we both knew it was coming. They were going to find out where you were sooner or later. You and I have been dating for approximately five minutes. My cousin and I can work something out. I know you like your space, and you're entitled to it."

"You should stay here," he said with a frown. "It's not like there isn't plenty of room. That way, keeping you safe and free from all of this will be easier."

"But—"

"Babe," he said. And that's *all* he said. The cranky, determined expression on his face did the rest of the talking for him.

"Guess we can see how it goes," I said. "At least your house has functioning air con."

"Yours isn't working?"

"No."

He rolled his thick shoulders and stared out the kitchen window. Then he asked, "Any chance I can convince you to take some time off work?"

"I'd rather not do that to Linda with no notice. They wouldn't really hassle me at the store, would they?"

"Oh my sweet child. The paparazzi have got your scent now," said Smith. "Or they will as soon as you stick your head out there. Is your cousin single?"

I poked a finger at him. "You stay away from my cousin, Smith. Her fiancé just dumped her in the middle of the apparently majestic Norwegian fjords. She doesn't need your kind of trouble."

"Harsh," he mumbled. "I make a great rebound."

"No."

"That's why you're here." Garrett shook his head. "Some girl you were seeing got too serious, so you decided it was time to get out of L.A. and go into hiding."

"I could have just missed you." Smith sniffed. "You were behaving like such a little bitch, you didn't even show me the whole house the last time I was here. I didn't even get to see the attic, and Grace assured me once that it was haunted. I might have just decided it was time for us to have a proper visit."

"You're so full of shit."

Smith leaned across the table toward me and said, "Thank goodness you're here, sweetheart. He has no manners. Whenever you're ready to run away with me, you just give me the word."

I smiled. "Duly noted. And stay away from my cousin."

Chapter Thirteen

DATING A ROCK STAR WAS WEIRD. IF THAT WAS WHAT WE were still doing. Monday morning found me at work with not one, but two bodyguards. Riley stood at the front door, monitoring the customers coming and going. While Van sat at a table with Linda, having his tarot read. He'd held out against her for as long as he could, bless him. But she'd worn the ex–special forces dude down in the end. Both bodyguards wore black slacks and a matching polo shirt. And their general alertness and the way they carried themselves . . . you would not want to mess with either of these people.

It was safe to say I no longer recognized my life. Just when I'd started to expand my security bubble, I wound up with bodyguards. Wild.

Garrett had spent the majority of Sunday in meetings. Another large helicopter had delivered security people, the band's manager and her assistant, their PR person, and lots of packages. Garrett, Smith, and the business folk disappeared into the office in the basement. I don't know what time the meeting finished. The assistant came up to fetch food and drinks a couple of times. But otherwise . . . nothing.

Eventually, I gave up and went to bed. When I woke for work, Garrett was curled around me, fast asleep. And all the while, the collection of media and fans at the gate kept growing. It was a lot to get my head around.

"If he hadn't pulled a Houdini and disappeared for two years, they wouldn't be so worked up," said Cézanne, sipping a decaf. "Not that he wasn't doing what was necessary to look after himself and deal with his grief. You know what I mean."

"I know what you mean."

"On the plus side, you look great."

"Thanks."

The bulk of the packages had been supplies for me. Whoever had organized same had not stinted on the spending. I had enough tampons and period products for the next year, three different skincare routines, a makeup collection to rival a Kardashian's, and over a dozen different outfits ranging from suitable for work to walking the red carpet, with underwear and accessories to match. Today, I was wearing an Alexander McQueen white ribbed halter-neck tank top, baggy blue jeans, and dark gray Chucks. It was ridiculous. I had to be the most expensively dressed grocery store clerk ever. I'd always wanted to be bougie, but never had the cash. Now was my time to shine.

When I had pointed out yesterday that one of the security people could have just gone next door and grabbed some of my stuff, Garrett smiled and said, "I like spoiling you. Get used to it."

All of a sudden, Cézanne's cell started beeping its heart out. She pulled it out of her purse with a sigh. "I set up an alert for your name."

"Shit."

A couple of media types had been in this morning for coffee. Neither had shown any interest in me until they noticed the bodyguards. The situation was its own self-fulfilling prophecy. At least the place was doing a roaring trade with all of the extra people in town.

"How bad is it?" I asked.

"They've got an old shot of you and Chad together," said Cézanne. "Which leads me to believe he's the asshole who spilled the beans."

I just shrugged.

"'Small-town girl heals Garrett's broken heart,'" said Cézanne. "Nice headline. They've only got your name and a brief rundown. The name of the town and where you work. About what you'd expect. Nothing too interesting yet."

"Don't read the comments."

"Oh hell no."

"Hey! Get away from me," shouted an irate young woman. She was being escorted to the door by Van. Her cell was pointed in my direction. Guess the picture of The Dead Heart on her tee kind of gave her interest away.

"And so it begins," intoned Linda.

Ugh. "I understand if you'd rather I take some time off. If you wanted to find someone else to work the counter during the weekdays. At least for a little while."

"We've already been over this."

"Yeah, but—"

"No." Linda waved the idea away, making her silver bangles clatter and clink. "You run this place. I only show up to drink a few pots of tea and visit with people. And that's the way I like it. Unless of course you're needing some time off to deal with all of this?"

I tried again. "No, but—"

"Van," she said. "I really feel like we need to explore your past lives more thoroughly. There are answers to be found there, I think."

The big man just nodded. "Whatever you say, ma'am. Just a little busy right now."

"Later is fine. And Ani, there'll be some of this boloney for a while, but so what? Eventually they'll move onto something new." Linda smiled benevolently. "The farmers and various suppliers all like dealing with you. There's no way I'm learning how to use that accounting software, either. No, thank you. You'll just have to stay."

"If you're sure."

"I'm sure. I've weathered storms before, dear. I believe if anything, they make life more interesting."

Cézanne just kept sipping on her decaf. "This should definitely be interesting."

My sudden fame/infamy wore thin by closing time. Though we had sold out of baked goods, bottled water, and other various items due to people making excuses to see me in the flesh. To take creeper shots with their cells. That sort of thing. All of the interest in me for bedding down with Garrett was beyond bizarre. Josh had hung out for a while, enjoying himself immensely. He tried charging tourists five dollars for a selfie. However, people lost interest fast when they found out the selfie was with him and not me.

What had been transpiring on the internet was best ignored. It wasn't like I could change anything. They would say and do what they pleased. And I did ignore the bulk of the bullshit. But I'd be a liar if I said none of it stung.

"The sheriff has been by a few of times," reported Riley on the drive home. Or rather, back to Garrett's house. "He and his deputies are helping to keep things calm."

The crowd had swollen in size. Guess it being summer holidays meant some of the Dead Heart fans had the free time to gather on our street. A couple of guards lingered at the front gate to make sure no one tried making a dash for the house. There were several big black Escalades and a sleek low white sports car parked by the door. More visitors, apparently.

I just needed to see Garrett. For reasons.

My bodyguards escorted me into the house, where someone was thrashing an electric guitar while another musician pounded out a beat on a set of drums. What else was a sitting room for? The music was so loud it made my ears ring. I didn't bother to try to identify the newcomers. But they radiated a general sense of rich and cool.

I, however, was on a mission. I went straight for the man himself. He stood sipping a beer amongst his guests with a small smile on his face. Like he was actually happy for a change. But a frown furrowed his brow at the sight of me. Though it might have been due to my own dubious expression.

"Can I see you for a minute, please? Now," I said, heading into the kitchen. Where the band's manager and her assistant were hard at work at the table. For fuck's sake. The security people had set up in the dining room, and I was not going upstairs. It was too far away.

So instead, I turned to him and said, "Get in the pantry."

"You want to talk in the pantry?"

"It's the closest and most convenient option for us to have a little privacy."

He frowned some more but did as told.

It was, all in all, a spacious pantry. But two people still made the space cozy. At least someone had done a decent grocery shopping and the shelves were no longer bare. I took his beer out of his hand, downed a mouthful, and then planted my face in the middle of his chest. He immediately wrapped his arms around me, and thank goodness for that.

"Ani, are you okay?"

"That was a day."

"What happened?" His expression couldn't be more thunderous. And his black eye had turned spectacular shades of purple and blue today. It was seriously impressive.

"Fans and so on coming into the store and staring at me and taking my picture without asking permission."

"Is that all?" He let out a sigh of relief. "You had me worried."

"I know it's normal for you, but it is not for me."

"I'm sorry." His arms tightened around me. "Will you tell me about it, babe?"

I downed some beer and ignored my hot, itchy eyes. "Grace's father called me a low-class yeehaw whore who could never replace his beloved daughter."

"Shit. I hadn't heard about that."

"I don't even know how to ride a horse. It makes no sense. But how lovely to have that splashed all over the inter webs."

He winced. "She hated her dad. Hadn't talked to him since she was eighteen. But that asshole always loved it when the media asked his opinion. Got real pissed when she didn't leave him anything in her will."

"I do not blame her for hating him one bit," I said. "Then your fans started coming into the store and wow, did they have some opinions. One of them said I was just some hot, fat bimbo and you'd get tired of fucking me in no time."

"Babe—"

"At least she called me hot. That was kind of nice."

He just frowned.

"Tell me something good."

He grabbed hold of my hips and rested his forehead against mine and took a deep breath. And another. "I missed you. Thought I would be able to go a day without you around. But I couldn't stop thinking about you. And there's definitely other shit going on right now that needs my attention."

I gave him a weary smile. "That's nice to hear."

"I was worried when you came in that you were going to tell me we're over. That it's all too much and you want to go home, or you want the bodyguards gone," he admitted. "That they were annoying you or something. The thought of anything happening to you terrifies me."

"Being here and having the bodyguards are fine. For now."

He licked his lips. "If we're going to do this, I cannot lose you too. You have to understand that. I can't go through that again."

"I know. I'm not going to take any unnecessary risks."

"Okay." He squeezed his eyelids shut for a moment. "That's good."

"I just really needed a hug. Like *really* needed one. From you, specifically."

He nodded. His hands had moved around to cupping my ass cheeks through the denim of my jeans. Then he hid his face in my neck and did some more deep breathing. "What's this?"

"Hmm?"

He lifted his head and snagged the platinum chain hanging around my neck. Nice and easy, he lifted the pendant out from where it had hidden underneath my top all day. "Is this real? Fuck. It is, isn't it? That's a big-ass diamond."

"Yeah, um . . ."

"Like really fucking large."

"I meant to talk to you about that. We can send it back, of course. I was just, you know, trying it on for size. Then I thought it might be safer on me than lying around the house. But it's not like we're up to the buying-expensive-jewelry stage of things," I babbled on. Talk about busted. "The expensive everything else was quite enough."

"I take it that came with all of the other stuff for you?" he asked, inspecting the solitaire round-cut rock.

"Yes. Thank you for organizing all of that, by the way."

"No problem. I wonder . . ." He shuffled us around and reached out to open the pantry door so he could holler, "Smith. Come here a minute."

A moment later, the big blond wandered on into the kitchen, cocking his head to see us through the partially open pantry door. "Why are you two hanging out in the cupboard?"

"I don't suppose by any chance that the latest woman you ran away from worked at our manager's office?"

Smith's gaze turned wary. "Why would you ask that?"

Garrett showed him the rock hanging around my neck.

"Huh. That's some sizeable bling."

"So you pissed this girl off, and she's using my money to somehow get back at you," said Garrett. "Is that about right?"

Smith tugged on his short beard. "It would seem that way, yeah."

"Because I asked them to send up anything Ani might need for the next few weeks. But I don't recall saying anything about them hitting up Harry Winston."

"Cartier," I corrected. "Not that I was going to keep it. Let me just reiterate that oh so salient fact. But I didn't think leaving it sitting around was a good idea and since I had the bodyguards, I thought . . . why not? Which I see now was a horrible, terrible decision."

"It's fine, babe," said Garrett. "Not your fault."

"You should keep it." Smith's expression was serious. "He can afford it. I mean, it can't be worth more than, say, a couple of hundred grand."

Garrett's brows rose high on his forehead.

"What?" asked Smith. "Are you really going to take it off her?"

I reached back to undo the clasp behind my neck and carefully handed the very expensive baby over. "He's not taking it off me. I'm giving it back."

Smith just frowned. "It looked pretty on you."

"Go away, man." Garrett slipped the necklace into his jeans pocket. Then he closed the pantry door and turned back to me.

Before he could speak, I said, "Might be worth checking through the rest and returning some other items, since it seems she might have gone a little overboard."

"It's fine."

"Are you sure?"

"No tiaras or swimming pools or anything else like that in there?"

"Not that I noticed," I said. "Just lots of expensive clothing and shoes and so on."

"Then no." He crowded me against the shelves with his big body. "Have at it."

"Are you sure?"

"Yeah."

"Okay." My smile was ever so slightly huge. "Thank you very much."

"So I've learned two important things today." Amusement lit his gaze. "One. You require regular hugging. Which I am happy to provide. And two. Whenever I fuck up, I can always try buying my way back into your good graces."

"Those are both good things to learn. But I would remind you that I'm also highly susceptible to your hugs, And they, compared to other items, don't cost the earth."

His mouth covered mine and his tongue swept in, and yeah. So much better. The way his hands covered my ass and kneaded. How he gave himself over to doing just this here with me. Kissing him made me high. Nothing else mattered.

Which was when a certain Great Dane started to scratch and sniff and whine at the outside of the pantry door.

"While I'd much rather stay here with you and make out, we better go," he said, placing a quick kiss on my lips. Then he said, "There's some people I want you to meet."

"About that . . . what's going on? Why are all these people here?"

He flashed me a smile. "I'm getting The Dead Heart back together."

Chapter Fourteen

"O H," I SAID WITH NO COOL WHATSOEVER. "YOU'RE LUCAS Moulin."

The dude seated behind the drum kit in the sitting room gave me a vague smile. It was of the kind you'd see on the cover of *Vogue*. Then he gave me serious side-eye. "This your new girl?"

"That's right," said Garrett, an arm slung around my shoulders. "This is Ani."

Lucas gave the arm side-eye, too. Then said in a flat, disinterested tone of voice, "Nice to meet you."

I said a whole lot of nothing.

He was in his late thirties, with cheekbones to die for, short blond hair, and green eyes. Both handsome and horrible in equal measures, apparently. Which was disappointing.

A look passed between Garrett and Smith.

It wasn't the first time people had behaved dubiously about Garrett and me. And it wouldn't be the last. People love their opinions. I didn't doubt what Chad had said about it being discussed around town. Wildwood was great. But there are jerks everywhere. And Garrett and I made for great gossip. He was rich and I was poor. He was world famous and I was nobody. It all made for great ammunition for the bitter, small-minded, and bored. Whatever.

"This is who the new songs are about, huh?" asked Lucas, keeping the beat all the while. "Guess I should thank her."

"It wouldn't be remiss," growled Smith. His fingers moved over the strings of a guitar, picking out a tune as if it were nothing. No more than an afterthought. "Unless you want to fuck off back to L.A. and your early retirement."

A muscle ticked in Garrett's jaw.

Lucas swore and said in a snide tone, "Fine. Yeah. Welcome to the family."

"Give me strength." Smith looked to heaven. "Ani darling, let me give you the backstory. Once upon a time, Lucas dated Grace before Garrett. But he fucked it up. Big time."

"It wasn't for long," said Garrett, rubbing my back. His smile was halfhearted. "They managed to keep it out of the media."

"He was the reason she swore off musicians?" I asked.

"One of them. Yeah."

Smith laughed. "A big fucking one of them. She didn't even want to invite him to the wedding.."

Lucas curled his upper lip in anger. But he didn't deny it and he didn't stop playing.

"Where was I?" asked Smith. "Oh, yeah. Grace and Garrett got married and Lucas was the loser. The end."

"That must have made things awkward," I said quietly. Maybe one day I'd meet someone who hadn't at least been half in love with Grace, but that day was not today. Clearly.

"Like you wouldn't fucking believe. To see him still clinging to that crush even now is some bullshit. Try not to take it personally, Ani babe."

Garrett sighed. "I said to call her by her name, man. Just her name. Why is that so hard?"

"Fuck this." Lucas let his drumsticks fly. "This isn't going to work. I'm out of here."

"Apologize," said Garrett, getting all up in the other man's face.

"Thought we talked all of this out a long fucking time ago."

"Not to me, you idiot. To her." And Garrett pointed at me.

Lucas's angry gaze lingered on my face before he turned away. "Shit. How can you replace Grace so easily?"

"Are you kidding me?"

"It's only been a couple of years. Grace was . . . fuck. She was special, man."

"Yeah. She was. And now she's gone." Garrett sighed. "But I'm still here, and I hope I have a lot of years of living ahead of me. I dragged my ass through every fucking day after she died. And you know it."

Lucas nodded, his brow furrowed. "I know. I'm not saying you didn't . . ."

"I loved her. I think we both did. But she's gone and we have to accept that."

"Fuck," said Lucas, his voice fervent and raw. "I never tried anything. I swear, I never disrespected—"

"I know you didn't. But you *are* disrespecting Ani, and that I won't allow." Garrett grabbed the other man by the scruff of the neck and stared into his eyes. "She makes me want to keep living. She makes me want to write songs and get up in the morning and go out and actually have a fucking life. I cannot overstate her importance to me. Do you understand?"

Lucas squeezed his eyelids shut. "Ani, I'm sorry."

"Okay," I said. "Apology accepted."

Smith gave me a wink.

"If you're getting the band back together," I said, "where is Adam?"

"He's going to be a tougher sell." Garrett flicked his dark hair back from his face.

"Two bits of good news," said the band's manager. Someone I still hadn't gotten around to meeting. She was a petite Asian woman wearing an orange power suit with a black Dead Heart tee and high heels. Talk about having an aesthetic. She was cool as all hell. "Adam's agreed to at least talk to you. But you have to go to him. He's set a time for tomorrow night. Which will fit with our meeting with the record label for lunch tomorrow."

"You're going out of town?" I asked.

"Yeah. Just for a little while." Garrett frowned. "What's the second bit of good news?"

"I'm Faye, by the way." The woman stuck out her hand for shaking. "Nice to meet you."

I shook her hand. "Hi. Ani."

"The second good bit of news is twofold," said Faye. "Joel Willet just proposed onstage during a show at the Troubadour to his quarterback boyfriend. Everyone is desperate for pictures of the happy couple and any wedding details. And songstress Aurora just threw her lead guitarist paramour out of their suite at the Beverly Hills Hotel for cheating. Bad news for her, but good news for us. You're no longer the most interesting story of the day. Not even remotely. I'd say we're about to see an exodus of paparazzi from the front gate."

"Good," said Garrett.

"Unless, of course, you change your mind about giving that interview."

Garrett gave a stiff shake of the head. "No. Not yet. When we're ready to announce the new album, maybe."

"Okay." She shrugged. "What about you, Ani?"

I frowned. "What about me?"

"No," said Garrett forcefully. "She stays out of it. I'll talk about certain private matters because it's part of keeping Grace's legacy alive. But Ani is kept clear of all this."

"Ani is in it whether you want her to be or not, G. She should work with the PR people." Faye crossed her arms over her chest. "Get a quick course in what not to say."

"I'm not commenting at all," I said. "We've been a couple for not quite forty-eight hours. This all feels very premature."

"Don't worry, babe," said Garrett with a wink and a smile. "We're still taking it slow."

"I don't believe you at all," I grumbled.

Faye raised a brow. "I hate to be harsh. But have you noticed who you're dating? He comes with a high-stakes, fast-paced lifestyle. And you're now a part of it."

"Faye, did you happen to notice where we are?" asked Smith with a smile. "This is Bigfoot country. I think it's safe to say that Garrett's changing the rules on all of that stuff. He wants to record an acoustic album and support it with a limited tour. The days of traveling the world for two years at a time are over. At least for now."

"Not a bad thing," said Lucas. "We did our first world tour

when I was twenty-five. I'm about to turn forty. You give me shit about early retirement, but honestly, the last two years were nice. I missed making music, but I could pass on living out of a suitcase for the foreseeable future."

Garrett tipped his chin in acknowledgment.

"Adam obviously feels the same, or he'd be *here* and not hiding out from his ex-wife behind tall fences in the Hollywood Hills."

"Who could have guessed he and Genevieve wouldn't last," said Smith sarcastically.

Lucas smirked. "Would have thought he'd be here because he needs the money after she took him to the cleaners in the divorce."

Rock stars were vicious gossips, apparently. You learned something new every day.

"At least we're not just starting out, dependent on live gigs and the streamers, getting paid six cents a quarter," said Smith.

Lucas snorted. "Amen."

"Back to business. We're older and wiser. I say we do it differently this time." Garrett picked up a guitar and started tuning it by ear. "What do you think?"

"How differently?" asked Faye in her no-nonsense tone. "What do you plan on actually telling the record company tomorrow? And how limited will this tour be?"

Smith grinned. "Trust us, Faye. It's all good."

"This is officially the longest and strangest first date ever," I said, closing the bedroom door behind me.

"Guess we are still on our first date, aren't we?" Garrett

wandered out of the walk-in wardrobe with a beat-up over-night bag. "Will you sleep here while I'm gone? Please? I like the thought of you in my bed."

"With the crowd out front hopefully calming down, I was thinking of heading home."

He frowned. "You were?"

"Yeah."

He was wearing a faded Led Zeppelin shirt today. And damn, did he make it look good. Blue jeans and sneakers completed the look. Was it weird that I missed his bare feet? Guess all of the people in the house had him feeling less casual and comfortable than normal. It was understandable. And there was every chance I was stealing the tee off him to wear while he was away.

"What?" he asked with a smile. Those smiles were still on the timid side, but they were coming a little easier every day.

"Nothing."

He stared at my gray Chucks. "Is your underwear the same color?"

"I noted that you told the person in charge of shopping about my good luck thing."

Dropping the bag on the floor, he walked around me and undid the small button at the back of my top. "Your bra is white."

"If it was gray it would be visible through the material, and that wasn't the look I was after. But rest assured, my panties do indeed match the color of my shoes."

"It's an addendum to the rule, the bra being a separate color."

"You could say that."

He placed a kiss to the exposed slip of skin. "Good to know."

"Such a vested interest in my lingerie."

"You're damn right," he said with a smile. "What say we check out that restaurant in Falls Creek you wanted to go to when I get back?"

"That would be lovely. If you think the superfans will have decamped by then."

"Now that they know I'm here, there might always be a couple around," he said. "I know it's a lot. But do you think you can get used to that?"

"Won't know unless I try."

"Being with me is kind of complicated, huh?"

I smiled. "One step at a time."

"Babe, if you want to go home, I understand. I had the air-con fixed today while you were at work, so that won't be a problem."

"You fixed my air-con while having meetings and putting your band back together?"

"I had it fixed. Yes."

"That's some pretty great multitasking, Garrett. Thank you."

"You're welcome." He started pulling up my top, inch by slow inch. The pads of his fingers traced across my belly before dipping a little lower. "How do you feel about being naked with me right now?"

"It's a yes from me."

The way his smile turned vaguely lecherous was thrilling. "Good. Toe off your shoes?"

"I can't—they're laced too tight."

Without another word, he dropped to his knees in front of me and dealt with them. The way he looked up at me with heat in his eyes made my insides clench in response. It had been a stressful few days. We could both use some relief.

"Way I see it, you've got a couple of choices," he said. "You can stay here with the benefit of the extra security I've got on the house and everything. I had the fridge filled and you're all set."

"I noticed the food fairies had visited the pantry."

"Looked like we were going to be feeding a lot of people in the near future."

"But they're all going back to L.A. with you now, right?"

"Temporarily. Apart from a couple of security people to keep an eye on the house, and your bodyguards." He unbuttoned my jeans and lowered the zipper. "I trust that's okay with you?"

"I know it's important to you. So no, it's not a problem. At least until we know things have definitely calmed down around here."

"Thank you," he said, tugging my jeans down my legs so I could step out of them. For a moment, he stared at the gray silk and lace panties with their Brazilian back. He even ran a finger along either side, beneath the waistband above my thighs. "They're very nice."

"You approve?"

"Oh yeah." He licked his lips and his gaze turned a little dazed. "What were we talking about?"

"Me moving back home."

"Right. Yeah. If it's what you want, then okay. It's not ideal, because your place isn't fenced. But we can make it work if we have to. What's important is that you're comfortable."

I threaded my fingers through his hair, brushing it back from his face. To be able to touch him like this was a gift. One I'd never get over.

"I'd rather you stayed here, of course," he continued. "You're safer here, and I happen to like knowing you're here."

"I just miss my stuff, you know?"

"Understandable." He thought the situation over for a minute and then he said, calm as can be, "Why don't we just move your things over?"

I froze. "What?"

"It's not like there isn't plenty of room."

I was not hyperventilating. That was someone else. There was, however, every chance I was having a heart attack. "Garrett, did you just ask me to move in with you?"

"Yeah," he said. "You being here just makes sense to me."

"You can't just ask me to move in with you."

"Why not?"

"Well . . . it's too soon, for starters. I've never even lived with a boyfriend before. This is like a really big thing."

He gazed turned amused. "Babe, your house is right next door. It's not going anywhere. If you decide you don't like it here or you get sick of me, you can just move back."

"What if you get sick of *me?*"

"I don't see that happening," he said. "Do me a favor and take that top off, will you?"

"Holy shit. I mean . . . fuck. You can't just do that."

"But I already did. Guess it's your turn to freak out. It kind of makes a nice change, really." He rose to his feet. "Deep breaths. That's it. You're okay."

"You think this is funny. But you can't just ask someone to move in when you've been with them for all of two days, Garrett."

"Who made that rule?" he asked. I tried to cover my face with my hands, but he set my palms on his chest instead. "I told you I knew what this was the other night."

"Yes. I heard you. And I agreed."

"Ani, what do you believe *this* is?"

"It's us being together and seeing if that works or whatever."

"That's what you thought I meant?"

My head nodded jerkily.

"No, babe," he said. "What it means is, I'm with you."

I frowned in confusion. "That's what I said. You just repeated what I said. That clarifies nothing."

"Yeah. But when you say it, it means having dinner on weekends and hanging out now and then, right?"

"Basically. That's what dating is."

"Did you really think I just asked you to dinner on a whim?"

"No," I said. "Not a whim, exactly. But I didn't think the meal would be served with a copy of the key to your house."

He gazed down at me all serene. "When I make my mind up about something, it tends to stick."

"What if the information leading to your decision changes?"

"Then I reassess. But nothing like that has happened here with us. And for the record, I don't think it's going to," he said. "Ever since the night I knocked on your door and you told me you didn't want a damn thing from me—all while not wearing a bra—I've started living again. You challenge me and care for me and do a whole lot more that you don't even realize."

"That's nice." I discreetly sniffled. "So what exactly does it mean when you say you're with me, then?"

"When I say it, it means I'm with you now and that's it for me," he explained. "We can take it as fast or as slow as you like. But either way, we make this work because it's what we want, right?"

"Right."

"Because I'm with you, and I'm not doing this shit half-heartedly, I don't mind if you move in today or in a couple of months' time. If you're more comfortable with that idea. Does that make sense?"

"Two days, Garrett. It's been two days." I waved two fingers in his face in demonstration. The man just shrugged. My mouth hung open in awe. "Wow. You're really not afraid of commitment."

"No."

"No," I agreed. "Not even a little. You're way more used to being in a relationship than me, aren't you?"

"Yes."

I sighed. "Right. That's going to take some getting used to. I was kind of the lone adult in the last relationship I was in. This is very different."

"I'd hope so."

"Mm."

And he continued to stand there, calm as can fucking be. "Moving in together would have come up sooner or later. Just so happens I'm fine with now and the situation seems to suit."

I took a deep breath and let it out slowly.

"Babe, we good here? You taking that top off and moving in or what?"

"I don't know. This is a lot. Shut up and kiss me."

At this, he did grin. And it was beautiful, breathtaking, all of those things. "Whatever you want."

His mouth covered mine, and hell yes. This was what I needed. When his fingers crept beneath the hem of my top and started tugging it up, I smiled and let him divest me of the item of clothing. He took a moment to stare at the Simone Perele molded lace bra and my breasts within. Then he reached around and undid the clasps. All while he backed me toward the nearest wall. Which wasn't far. My bra was tossed aside and he knelt before me once again.

"You don't want to use the bed?" I asked.

"No." He hooked his fingers in the waistband of my panties and dragged them down my legs. "It's too far."

"It's right there."

"Yeah. Too far. Do you trust me not to freak out mid-fuck this time?"

"I think you'll be just fine."

"I also happened to notice you like seeing me on my knees," he said with a certain glint in his eyes.

"Oh, really?"

"Yeah. Your pupils get all dilated. It's a big giveaway." He pushed my legs apart, widening my stance a little, then he lifted one and rested it over his shoulder. "You feeling steady?"

"I'm fine."

"Good," he said, and stuck two of his fingers in his mouth to wet them. My insides clenched at the sight. He angled his head just so and started teasing his tongue through the lips of my sex. The way it made me shiver. With his thumbs holding me open, he used the flat of his tongue next. Lapping me from back to front, leaving no part of me unloved. I grabbed two fistfuls of his hair and just hung on for the ride.

I had found in life that certain people could be horribly halfhearted about eating a woman. Garrett was not one of those people. He eased one finger into me, then two, fucking me nice and slow. It was maddening when I wanted more. Needed more. He sucked on my labia and teased my clit all the while like a professional. The rock star French-kissed my cunt with joy, making we wet and wanting. It wasn't long before I was riding his face. And the noise of approval and hunger he made was the sweetest sound I'd ever heard.

He hooked his fingers to rub at a sensitive spot inside of me and sucked on my clit. Every muscle in me from top to toe drew tighter and tighter. I was either going to come or break. There were no other options.

I gasped and came. The way it rushed through me lit up every part of my being. A sea of stars filled my vision. It was beautiful.

Garrett eased my leg off his shoulder and got to his feet. All while keeping a hand pressing to my middle to make sure I didn't fall over. Which I appreciated.

"You good?" he asked.

I just nodded. My ability to use words had left the building, apparently.

He tore his tee off over his head and wiped his mouth. Then he undid his jeans and pushed them down a ways to release his cock. It was impressively hard. Veins stood out in stark relief and blood flushed the head purple. He gave it a couple of hard strokes and gave me a hungry look. Seeing his jaw set with such determination made me weak in the knees and then some.

With one arm wrapped around my waist and another around my ass, he ordered, "Up. Wrap your legs around me."

It wasn't like I was going to argue. Or stop and think. Because sex with Garrett was always the best idea ever. And especially after today.

I wrapped my legs around his waist and my arms around his neck. He positioned the head of his cock at my entrance and snapped his hips. My spine hit the wall and my breasts jostled against his chest as he filled me to capacity. The feel of him so thick and hard inside of me was divine. He kissed me hard and furious and I tasted myself on his tongue. When he drew back, his gaze was full of lust and wonder.

"How could I ever get enough of you?" he asked. "I'll calm down in just a moment, I swear."

I frowned. "Why would you want to do that?"

"Babe," he said with a smile.

With one hand under my ass and the other cradling the back of my head, the man proceeded to fuck me senseless. The first time had a habit of being hard and fast with us, and that was fine. There would be time to linger and be gentle later. But first we had to meet the voracious need for each other. To become one sweaty, messy tangle. Thank fuck we both felt the same way.

He dragged out the long length of his cock before pushing back inside. Setting a steady rhythm, building in speed. When he found the right spot to hit deep inside of me, a surprising one that made me gasp, his smile amped up to a grin.

"I can't again," I puffed.

"Sure you can."

With confidence like that, I never stood a chance. Especially since he had the skills to back it up. Once, twice, three times he worked the spot. And somewhere between four and five, I came. All of the delicate muscles inside of me clamped down on him and a release of happy chemicals burst through my brain. I bit his shoulder to stop from crying out his name. Or worse, saying something stupid like "I love you."

He groaned and bucked against me, burying his cock deep and coming hard. We were slumped against the wall with me wrapped around him like a howler monkey. Who was I kidding? Even with the biting, I had probably sounded like one too. When it came to this man, I apparently had no shame.

"Oh, shit," I said. "We didn't use a condom again. I brought some home. They're in my purse downstairs. I better make an appointment with the doctor and get on some birth control."

"Sounds sensible. Let me know if you want me to go with you."

"Okay."

"Will you move in?" he asked in a voice both gentle and lazy. "Please?"

"Oh, all right. But this is seriously not slow. Like . . . not even a little."

He pressed a kiss to my cheek. "Thanks, babe."

Chapter Fifteen

ARRETT AND THE GUESTS WERE GONE WHEN I WOKE THE next morning. They had gotten a seriously early start on the trip back to L.A. It was just me, my bodyguards, and some security people left. Which was still a lot of people. But my romance novels were now piled up beside our bed, my clothes hung alongside his in the walk-in wardrobe, and my favorite coffee mug sat in the kitchen cupboard. We were really doing this. This being the meshing of our lives and stuff. It was all both wild and wonderful at the same time.

My days of playing it safe in all the ways were in the rear-view mirror, apparently. Look at me taking chances on love. If I had made Garrett want to get out there and live again, the truth was, he'd done no less for me.

"They're going to start sleeping in your cabin?" asked Josh, waiting on his first coffee of the day at the general store. "Because I was thinking I could rent out my spare room at a tidy profit. There's only my mother's sewing machine, a Peloton, my old mountain bike, a Christmas tree, and the six-foot aquarium setup from when I used to have a pet turtle in there. It'd be a little cramped, but still very comfortable. You'd just have to bring your own beds and so on."

"Thank you, Josh," said Riley with an excellent blank face. "But I think we'll stick to the cabin for now."

He tossed back his mullet. "Suit yourself. You don't know what you're missing out on. I am damn fun to hang out and watch TV with. Just ask my wife. We're doing a David Attenborough binge this weekend. It's going to be great."

"You moved in with Garrett?" Linda clasped her hands together with a smile. "What wonderful news, Ani. Congratulations."

"Thanks," I said with an uneasy smile. "I'm still getting used to the idea."

"You're following your heart and it's wonderful to see."

"I'm going to pray for you both." And they did. "I hope that everything works out for you two."

"Thank you," I said.

After the rush yesterday, Heather was working with us. Along with being the judge of Tuesday Trivia Night, Heather had started working casual hours at the general store. She was a Black middle-aged woman with box-braids, a no-nonsense demeanor, and brilliant skill as a potter. We sold some of her beautiful mugs and bowls in the store. She and Linda could happily debate spiritual matters for days.

Though as Faye had predicted, there'd been a mass exodus of paparazzi. And most of the fans left when news of Garrett, Smith, and Lucas appearing in L.A. hit social media. This was followed by pictures of Garrett at Grace's grave site with a huge bouquet of roses. He hid his black eye behind sunglasses. He hadn't said anything about making the visit. But it made sense that he would go there. It was not a big deal.

The note I'd found on the kitchen table, however, was.

Van was on the door that day while Riley wandered the store. Both were minding their own business. Now was the time to talk it through.

"Garrett seems happy here, right?" I asked. "I mean, he bought up half the town. He must have plans to hang around at least for a while."

Linda cocked her head. "Why do you ask, dear?"

"Oh, nothing." I forced a smile. "Just thinking out loud."

Josh picked up his coffee. "Gary's happy as a pig in mud. We've been talking about starting a poker night. Imagine all the money I'm going to win off of him."

"But you're terrible at cards," said Heather.

"Nonsense. That's just negative talk." Josh headed for the door. "See you later!"

"Why is that frown on your face?" asked Linda with concern.

"Okay," I started. "I found a pros-and-cons list about Wildwood this morning in Garrett's handwriting, and I need to talk about it before my brain combusts. But it has to stay with us, okay?"

"Of course," said Heather. "It certainly seemed like the boy was settling in. At least, that's what everyone's been saying. I'm surprised to hear he's thinking of leaving."

"Right?" I pulled the piece of paper out of my pocket. "I don't understand. He hasn't mentioned any of this to me and we just made a massive commitment to one another and moved in together. It's confusing as all hell. I mean, Wildwood is my home. I'm happy here. I don't want to leave. I knew he'd be doing some travel for his work, but this is . . . shit."

"What's on it?"

"It's not actually that long. I think he was only getting started," I said. "But the pros are kind people, location, trivia night, and slower lifestyle. I had no idea he was interested in joining our trivia team. That's cool. While the cons are location and no nightlife."

Linda sighed. "The bar and grill is great. But I do have to admit that I miss nightclubs and jazz bars occasionally."

Heather just nodded.

"What am I going to do if he wants to move back to L.A.?" I wrapped my arms around myself.

"You need to talk this through with him, and the sooner the better," said Linda.

"Yeah, but I don't want to do it over the phone. This is more of a face-to-face, serious type of discussion. And he's busy with meetings and all sorts of things down there."

"He wouldn't want you stuck here worrying, dear."

"When is he back?" asked Heather.

"Tomorrow." I nodded. "I'll wait to talk to him then. I think that would be best."

The first text from him came at nine that night while I was lying on the bed, reading a book.

Garrett: Sorry, babe. This is taking longer than I thought. A few more days at least.

Me: Ok.

Garrett: Been stuck in meetings all day. Record company wining and dining us. Will call you tomorrow.

Garrett: Are you ok?

Me: Yes. All good. Talk to you tomorrow. x

Garrett: I miss you.

Me: I miss you too.

When Harry Met Sally is my mom's favorite movie. So I've seen it a time or six. There's a scene in the film where the hero has a moment of realization. When he runs across town on New Year's Eve at the stroke of midnight to tell the heroine the news. How he gets it now. How he's no longer afraid. She is his special one-in-a-million person, he knows it with all his heart, and he needed to tell her straight away so they could start their life together. I'd always thought it beautiful, but I don't know that I quite understood. Not until now.

I lasted a whole hour and a half before knocking on the door of the cabin next door. Riley answered in their pajamas, a star-covered onesie. "Miss Bennet, you shouldn't have left the house without contacting us first."

"I know. And I fully realize it's the middle of the night and I'm acting slightly ridiculously. But I need to go to L.A."

They just blinked.

"Now. Please?"

"You got it." They turned and yelled, "Van, get your ass out of bed. We're going on a road trip."

I liked to think I was a cool, calm, and rational woman. It obviously wasn't true, but I liked to think it just the same. With traffic, it was a twelve-hour trip to L.A. I offered to take my turn driving, but Van and Riley both vetoed the idea. Which left me curled up on the backseat of the Range Rover, staring out the window and thinking deep thoughts. My fingers kept tracing the old scar on the side of my neck. It had healed well for the most part. One day I might even stop hiding it.

The last time I'd done this trip, it had been in reverse and bad. A bare month after the attack, my life was a wreck. Both my job and my boyfriend were history and I was running home to hide. This time, I was running toward a possible bright future with everything I had in me.

People need to talk more about how love makes you stupid. How it makes you do wild and ridiculous things. Because four days into this relationship and here I was, traveling through the night to reach him. To ask him how and where he planned on spending, oh, say, the rest of his life. And how I was okay with moving if that was what would make him happy. Because I realized now that he was my heart and where he went, I would follow. One way or another, we'd work it out together.

Once we hit L.A., traffic was horrible, of course. There'd been discussions about flying from San Francisco to L.A., but Van and Riley had been wary of taking that route without more preparation time. I highly doubted people were that interested in me, but I didn't want to get them into trouble, either. And this all felt like a silly romantic road-trip kind of thing, what I was doing. I stared out at the view, watching trees and mountains turn into businesses and buildings.

The buildup of houses and people was . . . whoa. After four years of happily hiding out in the hills, it was intense. City life had lost none of its hustle or bustle. Not even at some stupid hour of the morning. A long time ago, my dream had been to own a place at Venice Beach. To be able to walk down to see the ocean whenever I liked. The thought of going home when I'd spent so long dreaming of leaving the small town had been dire. Things changed. Now I loved living in Wildwood. I appreciated the community.

But if Garrett wanted to return to the city, I would go with him. Assuming he wanted me with him, of course.

Chateau Marmont was a glamorous old hotel in West Hollywood with a storied history. From Britney Spears being banned to Dennis Hopper throwing orgies, John Belushi dying, and John Bonham riding a motorcycle through the lobby, it had it all. It was a seven-story white castle-like building towering over Sunset Boulevard. Security knew we were coming. But no one, including myself, had been able to get hold of Garrett. I was doing my best not to let that freak me out. After all, he was probably just sleeping soundly alone in his own bed or something like that. I trusted him. It would be fine.

The car pulled up at the front entrance, and Van and Riley rushed me through to a lobby and bar area where there were large arched windows and wood beams overhead. Lots of comfortable plush sofas and seats and a grand piano. And several guests giving me curious looks while I hunched over and caught my breath.

"Ani, is that you?" Lucas Moulin strode toward me carrying what appeared to be a Mimosa. "Looking for Garrett?"

I nodded.

"Did he know you were coming? Are you supposed to be here?" His handsome face turned distinctly cranky. "I don't remember him saying anything about you joining us. We've got a meeting with a big-name producer soon. None of us can miss it, you know?"

I glowered at the man. "Lucas, I'm not going to get in the way of any meetings. That's not why I'm here."

"Then why the hell are you here?"

"None of your business."

"It's definitely my business. If you pull some fuckery with Garrett that flows onto the band, you know?"

"Ugh. No. Go away. I didn't spend all night in the back of a car to take shit from you." I turned to Riley with a much calmer demeanor. "Do you know what room he's in?"

"So you do have teeth." Lucas smiled. "Good. You'll need them, new girl. Follow me."

Up to the top floor we traveled. Where Lucas hammered on the door with nil interest for his fellow guests staying in the hotel. "G!" he yelled. "Open the fucking door."

Garrett threw the door open with his hair disheveled and a pair of jeans with the zipper only half done up on his hips. "The fuck is your problem, man?"

"Your girl's here." Lucas took another sip of his cocktail and a step back from the door. "Don't forget we're out of here in forty minutes. Butch won't hang around if we're late."

"Ani?"

"Hey," I said with a weak smile. "Sorry for turning up out of the blue like this."

Then I was in his arms and everything was a whole lot better. Like instantly. "Are you okay? Is everything all right?"

"I need to tell you something real quick, then I'll go and you can get back to focusing on your meetings."

"Come on in." He nodded to Van and Riley before shutting

the door behind us. "I noticed all of the messages from security and Faye on my phone. I take it that's about you coming down here? I turned off my cell and crashed hard last night. But I'm here now. Talk to me."

Inside, the penthouse suite had a checkerboard-floor hallway and spacious rooms. At the end was a living area filled with more lush furniture, leading out to a balcony covered by a striped awning and expansive views of the city. It was impressive. But cool lodgings were not why I'd hauled ass across the state. I could do this—take the ultimate leap of trust in this man. He was worth making changes for. He was worth taking chances.

"Okay. The truth is, I may have freaked out just a little," I said. "But I swear I have good reason."

"Of course you do. What's wrong?"

"Nothing's wrong. I just had a realization. Kind of a profound one. It involves this . . . I found it after you left." I pulled the list of pros and cons out of my jeans pocket. "And I couldn't wait any longer to talk to you about it face-to-face. Sorry for barging in, by the way. Did I say that already? My mind's a bit scattered."

He frowned at the piece of paper.

"I've been thinking about it all night as we drove here," I said, taking a deep breath. It was time to pull up my big-girl panties. "And if you don't want to stay in Wildwood, if you want to come back to L.A., then I'm okay with that. I mean, I'd like to come with you. If that's what you want, of course."

"You would leave Wildwood for me?"

I nodded. "Yes."

"But you love it there."

"Yeah. I really do." I swallowed hard. "But I love you more."

"You love me?" His gaze gentled. "Even though this is only day five together?"

"Even then."

"Thank you," he said, pressing a kiss to my forehead. "I really appreciate that. Just so happens I love you too."

My smile was one of relief. "You do?"

"I went and told her about you, you know."

"You mean Grace?"

"Yes." He tucked a strand of hair behind my ear and smiled. "I visited her grave and told her that I'd found someone and was happy again. That I was as gone on you as I could be. And I said goodbye. It felt more real this time somehow than it did at her funeral. More final somehow."

"Okay."

"Not to say I'll never go back there. That's not what it was about. But I feel like things are actually moving on, and that's a really good thing."

"I'm glad."

His arms went back around me and he rested his chin on the top of my head. Touching him was so good. The warmth of his bare chest and the scent of him fresh out of bed. He was home now, and I was fine with the fact. Guess we'd both found our peace. Our hope for the future.

"I know you have an important meeting to get to. But you haven't actually told me," I said. "Are we moving to L.A. or what?"

"And get city soft? What would Josh say?"

I laughed. "He'd be appalled."

"Linda would be outraged if I stole you from her. And Cézanne's having a baby. You know you want to be there for that."

I drew my brows together and looked up at him, all curious. "Wait. So we're not moving?"

"Babe, that list was for Smith. Not me. He's thinking about making some changes and wanted to talk it through."

"Oh. Shit." My eyes were wide as can be. "I got all worked up and came here for nothing."

"Not for nothing. I happen to like having you with me. I like it even more when you travel all this way to tell me you love me for the first time. That's pretty fucking important as far as I'm concerned."

I cuddled him tighter, just because I could. My life was awesome like that. "Smith's thinking of moving to Wildwood and joining the trivia team. I did not see either of these things coming."

"Yeah. I guess so." He smiled. "I have no interest in moving back here anytime soon. You can have a big-ass mansion in the hills here if you like. But I'm happy with where we are. In fact, I'm planning on recording the album at the house. It'll involve a lot of people coming and going and guests staying for a while. But it means we can both be exactly where we want to be."

"I love this idea, Garrett. This is excellent news."

"Good."

"Wow." I sighed. "We're staying in Wildwood."

The light in his eyes and smile on his face were so pure and true and uncomplicated. "Yes, we are. It's our home, right?"

"Right. Now I need to go and let you get back to business."

"No, babe. Crash here for the day. We can head back tonight, if you like," he said. "Or I could take you out for a few drinks at Soho House. We could even catch Stage Dive at the Hollywood Bowl."

KYLIE SCOTT

I thought it over. "That does sound fun."

"Or we could do it another time." He smiled. "When you haven't spent the night in a car traveling the country."

"Home does sound awfully good."

"Home it is."

"But first . . ."

I reached up and pressed my lips against his. The man immediately took the hint and kissed me back. His hands in my hair and his breath mingling with mine. It was all good.

Given how he'd been so understanding about my latest freak-out, I was feeling particularly amorous. Also with the way he loved Wildwood like me. And the way his side of the bed had been empty last night. My chest was packed full of warm, fuzzy feelings in general. Like my heart had grown a size or two. This had to be what feeling supported by and safe with your partner was like. Can't say I'd ever had it before. Friends and family were great. But this was special too.

I happy-sighed. "How much time do we have before you have to go?"

"Not long, unfortunately," he said. "But we can be quick."

"Oh, you want to . . ."

"Yes."

I slid my hands down his stomach and lowered the zipper on his jeans all the way. He broke the kiss and watched me with heated eyes. Such delicious smooth skin against my palms as I inched his jeans down over his hips. Just far enough to free his cock. Such a splendid organ. Seriously.

I smiled and got to my knees.

"Fuck," he muttered.

I wet my lips and got busy. He wasn't fully hard yet. I could

214

fit most of him inside my mouth. At least at first. With tongue and teeth, I teased him. One hand massaging his balls while the other took charge of his burgeoning hard-on. As he got harder and thicker, I pulled back, focusing on the crown. And all the while he watched me without blinking. Like he didn't want to miss a thing.

The scent of him filled my head and the taste of salty precum hit my tongue. I gave his hard length a firm stroke. Tracing the ridge around the head of his cock, digging the tip of my tongue into the sensitive indent underneath. His breathing started coming faster and the muscles in his stomach and thighs tensed. Getting to be this close and do these things to him. To have him however I liked. How great was that?

"That's enough," he said, taking a step back.

"No, it's not."

"Let me show you something. First thought I had when I walked into this room, and it was all about you." With his hands beneath my arms, he lifted me to my feet and directed me to a long nearby table. Then he pulled a couple of chairs out and ushered me forward. His hand gently pressing against my back, urging me to bend over. "Look at the wall, babe."

"Huh. That's a very large mirror."

Talented fingers undid my pants and pushed them and my panties down to my ankles. With his foot, he widened my stance. As far as the shackles of my clothing would allow. His hands smoothed over my wet cunt and he smiled at me in the mirror. There were a lot of sharp teeth in that smile. Here was a man about to take a bite out of me. And I couldn't wait.

After further wetting his cock head with saliva, he lined himself up with my opening and asked, "We good?"

"Um. Yeah."

A snap of the hips and he impaled me on his thick length. All while I watched him in the mirror. His dark hair fell forward over his face, but his hungry gaze never left me. The way my insides quaked around him. He gripped my hips tight, fucking into me sure and true.

I didn't recognize myself. The girl with dazed eyes sprawled across the table taking it from behind was a stranger to me. But this was my life now. This was where I belonged. Sex with rock stars in luxury penthouses was my thing now, apparently. And it blew my little mind.

Garrett leaned over me, shoving a hand up the front of my shirt to grasp hold of a breast. The fervor in his eyes and the thrusts of his cock had me trembling. It was in the skilled and proprietary way he handled me. How he fucked with such stamina and skill. This was my man. My person. I have no idea how I got this lucky. But I was never letting go.

"There we are," he said. That's you and me. See how good we are together?"

I could only nod.

His teeth grazed my spine. "You need to catch up, babe."

His hand reversed direction and slid down my front to play with my clit. Rubbing circles and driving me wild. He had me gasping in no time. It was like my insides turned upside down and inside out. The heat of our combined bodies and the thrill flowing through me. How it all centered in my sex and felt so fucking fine. I convulsed around him as he gritted his teeth and came.

I collapsed on the table and he rested against my back, both of us working hard to catch our breath. His fingers swept up and down my side, beneath my shirt.

"You don't ever have to apologize for coming and finding me," he said. "I always want you with me, okay?"

"Okay," I agreed with a smile.

He lifted my hair and placed a kiss at the back of my neck. "Let me go deal with these last few meetings, babe, and then we can go home."

Chapter Sixteen

T O CELEBRATE OUR ONE-MONTH ANNIVERSARY, THE DEAD Heart were playing a set at the Wildwood Bar and Grill. Though, to be honest, it was mostly about trying out their new songs on a small audience. Having the band ease back into performing live together, since it had been a while. Emma and Yong were ecstatic for the extra business. While organizing the security and so on had been hard work, all of the locals were excited to see the show.

It also coincided with the opening of the new ice cream shop, a clothing boutique, and the relocation of Magda's hair-dressing salon. Claude and Lupe's diner was another week away. The town library was well on its way to being restored to its former book-lending glory. The movie theater would take a while yet due to extensive damage done by time, neglect, and the weather. But one day we might watch movies on the big screen once more.

Back to the here and now . . . Lucas's girlfriend, country singer Jessie Moore, was busy signing napkins and scraps of paper at the bar. If the girl flipped her long blond hair one more time, she might do her neck some damage. All of the fawning admiration from local fans suited her just fine.

You might have collected from my tone that she and I did not get along, and you'd be right. Even my new amazing life had some hiccups.

As anticipated, there'd been plenty of people coming and going at home in the last two weeks since recording started. There were several Airstreams parked in Garrett's yard, with more next door at my old place. They housed a certain member of the band and his plus-one, the producer, the guitar tech, a couple of sound techs, and various security people. Faye and a dude from the record company came and went too.

Miss Therese had refused to evict the various contractors working on Main Street just because some big-name music industry types wanted a room. Not even when they offered to pay extra. And good on her. Garrett had told them they were fools to ask, but they wouldn't believe him.

Lucas and Jessie had lasted one whole day in the house before being evicted. Due in large part to Jessie acting like an ass and refusing to pick up her shit. The bathroom floor had been covered in wet towels, makeup wipes, and other assorted detritus after she'd spent two hours enclosed in the space perfecting her look. She was saddened to find out that I wasn't in fact her maid. Not even a little. And Garrett had zero tolerance for the way she talked down to me. We now ignored each other, which worked great.

Smith had decamped early on to the battered wooden A-frame he'd convinced Mr. Akana to sell him. It was just down the road. Guess Smith had decided to at least attempt spending some time in Wildwood. I had returned his list to him, and he smiled and declined to discuss same. But here he was, a local homeowner. Some of the Main Street contractors were working with him on fixing up the place when they had the time. Whether he stayed on once the album was finished was yet to be seen.

The mysterious bass player, Adam, had gone with Smith. He was a tall, lanky, dark-haired guy who had put out his own album during the band's hiatus. And it had done well for him. Like Smith, he in general seemed lighthearted. Less prone to the intense brooding Garrett used to indulge in and Lucas still held dear. Though any mention of his ex-wife, Genevieve, tended to send Adam into a sullen silence.

Men. They were such delicate creatures.

What I loved about them recording at home was getting to hear the songs come together. Hearing Garrett's voice go from whiskey-smooth to rough and raw and back again. I could listen to him sing for hours. And I often did. "Sunshine" and "Lost and Found" were my favorites of their new songs. I had never had songs written about me or around me before. Both experiences were amazing. As was watching The Dead Heart work.

The whole band were consummate professionals when it came to laying down the tracks. Even Jessie stopped her prima donna crap long enough to provide backup vocals on a song. Everyone in the band contributed to the writing. Adam and Garrett seemed to be the main suppliers of lyrics. But everyone worked on the music together most of the time.

Half of the album was done. Tonight they'd play for Wildwood. Party lights were strung up above the stage and everyone was dressed in their Sunday best for the occasion.

At least, there were no holes in Josh's jeans and his mullet was freshly washed and styled. It was a high compliment for him to pay the band, considering his disdain for rock 'n' roll. Though maybe he did it to impress Jessie.

And none of this went toward explaining why I was in hiding when the band were about to go onstage. In the Wildwood Bar and Grill bathroom. As you do.

Like the main room, it was all wood, with three stalls and white pedestal basins from the '50s. Old, but clean. I sat on the random chair placed in the corner. In all likelihood, it was intended as a resting place for drunk girls. Or for women to put their purses on while they washed their hands. I don't know. But right now, my butt rested on its aged surface and I stared at the floor and tried to keep my cool.

Cézanne stood nearby, with a hand smoothing over her tiny baby bump. She said nothing. There was nothing left to say. But I appreciated her support just the same. I'd already been on Cézanne's phone to Maria earlier. We'd had a long and involved three-way conversation. Truth was, I had a damn great support team to see me through the ups and downs in life.

Now I just needed to talk to the other person this situation truly affected. Once he'd finished his show. I wouldn't load him up with stress when he was about to go onstage.

Only the door opened and Garrett strode inside. "Babe. You okay?"

"Hey," I said with relief and a shaky smile. "What are you doing here? I thought you guys were about to start?"

"I saw you come in before and you didn't come out. Is everything okay?"

Cézanne gave me a nod and headed for the door. Garrett and I were alone.

"Hey. What happened at the doctor's?" he asked, squatting in front of me. He was in full rock-star mode. Black jeans, matching button-down shirt, boots on his feet, and half his hair tied back in a man bun. He was so beautiful. He really was my whole damn heart. I just hoped he felt the same. "You took a while."

"Yeah, I um . . . there was a wait. The doctor had to go out to the Miller's farm for an emergency. Mrs. Miller pulled something in her back and got stuck under a tractor she'd been fixing. My cell died or I would have texted you that I'd been held up. Sorry."

"That's okay. You're here now. How did the appointment go?"

"Um. Yeah. It went."

He did the frown/smile thing that was now his go-to look. It was a kind of confusion. Whenever he wasn't sure what was going on, but didn't want to be negative, he made that face. "I'm going to need you to give me a little more information. What does that mean?"

"I was waiting to talk to you about all this after the show."

He narrowed his gaze on my face. "Hmm," he said. "How about you talk to me about it now instead?"

"Are you sure?"

"Yeah."

"All right." I squared my shoulders. "Before he would put me on any birth control, he asked me to do a pregnancy test. Just to be sure."

"Right."

"It's pretty standard procedure, apparently."

Garrett nodded.

My mouth opened, but nothing came out. It was approximately the third time I'd broken out in a cold sweat in the last half hour or so. No deodorant stood a chance of keeping up with me.

"Are you pregnant?" asked Garrett. "Is that what you're having trouble telling me?"

I nodded jerkily. "It's very early days, but ah . . . yeah."

"Okay." His forehead furrowed. "We did kind of push the bounds of safe sex there for a while at the start."

My hesitant smile was at least half wince. "Right? Who could have known there'd be possible consequences?"

"How do you feel?"

"Wait. Tell me first. Are you mad?"

"No," he said, voice adamant. "Of course not."

I wrung my hands in my lap. "I just . . . we did start using condoms and I thought . . ."

"That we'd been careful enough with the timing." He grabbed hold of my hands. "I know, babe. We're both adults. We both knew the risks we were taking."

"Then I thought I was just late. So much has been going on lately and I have been a little stressed. Mostly with all the mayor stuff."

"Do you have any idea about what you want to do?"

I breathed out slow and easy. "Garrett, it's our baby."

"Yeah."

"We barely even talked about maybe having a family. I know this is a lot sooner than we might like, but . . . I want to."

KYLIE SCOTT

"Are you sure?" he asked. "You know I'll support you, whatever you decide."

"I'm sure. My mind's made up."

"Okay." His slow smile was everything. And it just kept on spreading. The delight in his eyes was wild. "We're having a baby. I'm going to be a father. Fuck. This is amazing."

I could have burst into tears, I was so damn relieved. He was happy. I was with child. I sort of wanted to throw up, but it was all going to be fine. "You really are fine with this."

"I'm fucking thrilled," he said. "Before I came here I was alone. I thought for sure I wouldn't be starting a family ever. You, babe, are the gift that keeps giving. And I couldn't be more grateful."

"Wow." I laughed. "I see you're still really not afraid of commitment?"

"Not when it comes to you and ours." He stood, drawing me up with him. "I knocked up the mayor. How about that. Think they'll give me a plaque or name a park after me?"

"I'd be outraged if they didn't." I let out a breath I'd been holding for approximately forever. Or at least since Doc Singh told me the news. "I love seeing you happy."

"You were really worried, huh? Come on," he said. "Let me show you something I planned earlier. It might make you feel a little better about this surprise."

"What?"

He grinned. "Just come on."

Back out into the bar we headed, before making an abrupt turn toward the stage. Where the guys were tuning their instruments and waiting. The place was packed, as you'd imagine. But Garrett didn't leave me in the crowd with Linda and Cézanne

224

and Mike. Nope. He didn't even give me a chance to introduce my cousin Astrid, who was hanging out by the bar. Instead, he dragged me up the couple of steps onto the stage and went for his microphone. With me in tow.

"Good evening," he said. Every head in the bar turned in our direction. Cheers and applause filled the room. "One small but important piece of business before we start tonight's show."

"What is it, Gary?" asked Claude, who stood with his arm around Lupita.

Without further ado, Garrett fished a ring out of his front jeans pocket. Then he took hold of my left hand and said quietly, "It doesn't have to go on your ring finger. This can be a commitment sometime down the track if that's what you're more comfortable with. But I would very much love to put this on your ring finger and set a date sometime if you're amenable."

"That diamond is even bigger than the pendant."

"I know. I wanted this to be the first rock I gave you."

"You've been planning this that long?"

"Pretty much," he said. "I told you I knew what I was getting into. What do you say?"

Smith stuck his big blond head in beside mine. "Say it's a commitment ring, Ani darling. That way he has to buy you another, even fancier one when you actually get engaged. Think of all the bling you'll have then. You'll be dripping in stones."

Garrett just shook his head.

I gave it approximately a second's thought and held out my ring finger. The cheers and applause were loud. He slipped the large square-cut diamond and platinum ring on my finger. Then he cupped the back of my neck and pulled me in for a kiss. A long and deep one. I clung to his shoulders, refusing to let go for an instant.

"You said yes," he said with a smile. "That's pretty brave."

"We're doing this." I shrugged. "I love you. Of course I said yes."

"I love you too, babe. So much. Why are you crying? This is a good thing." With the side of his thumb, he wiped a tear off my face. And together, hand in hand, we turned to face the gathered citizens of our fair town. All of the familiar faces sharing in our special moment. I wouldn't want it any other way.

Beside me, Garrett stood happy and whole. He raised my hand with the ring on it to the crowd and said, "Thank you, Wildwood. Really. You gave me a new life. You gave me love. Thank you for everything."

The crowd went wild.

Continue reading for a sneak peek of

Fake

Chapter One

H E SLUNK INTO THE RESTAURANT MID-AFTERNOON wearing his usual scowl. Ignoring the closed sign, he took a booth near the back. No one else was allowed to do this. Just him. Today's wardrobe consisted of black jeans, Converse, and a button-down shirt. Doubtless designer. And the way those sleeves hugged his biceps . . . why, they should have been ashamed of themselves. I was this close to yelling "get a room."

Instead, I asked, "The usual?"

Slumped down in the corner of the booth, he tipped his chin in reply. For such a tall guy, he sure went out of his way to try to hide.

I said no more. Words were neither welcomed nor wanted. Which was fine since (A) I was tired and (B) he tipped well for the peace and quiet.

Out back, Vinnie the cook was busy prepping for tonight, his knife making quick work of an onion.

"He's here," I said.

A smile split Vinnie's face. He was a huge fan of the man's action films. The ones he'd made before hitting it big time and taking on more serious dramatic roles. Him choosing to visit the restaurant every month or so made Vinnie's life complete.

Especially since the restaurant, Little Italy, was the very defini-
tion of a hole in the wall. Not somewhere generally frequented
by the Hollywood elite. Meanwhile, I was less of a fan, but still
a fan. You know.

"Get him his beer," Vinnie ordered.

Like I didn't know my job. Sheesh.

He was busy with his cell by the time I placed the Peroni in
front of him. No glass. He drank straight from the bottle like an
animal. Just then, a woman in a red sweater dress and tan five-
inch-heel booties strode in through the front door.

"I'm sorry, we're closed," I said.

"I'm with him." She headed straight for his booth and slid
into the other side, giving the man a dour look. "You can't just
walk out, Patrick. You're going to have to choose one of them."

"Nope." He took a pull from his beer. "They all sucked."

"There had to be at least one that would do."

"Not even a little."

She sighed. "Keep this up and you'll be obsolete by next
week. Beyond help. Forgotten."

"Go away, Angie."

"Just another talented but trash male in Hollywood. That's
what they're saying on social media."

"I don't give a shit."

"Liar," she drawled.

I wasn't quite sure what to do. Obviously they knew each
other, but he did not seem to want her here. And she really
wasn't supposed to be here. Vinnie had okayed after-hours entry
to only one person. On the other hand, if I asked her to leave,
she'd probably sic her lawyers on me. She looked the type.

The woman spied me hovering. "Get me a glass of red."

"She's not staying," countermanded Patrick.

Angie didn't move an inch. "They were all viable options. Pliant. Young. Pretty. Discreet. Nothing weird or kinky in their backgrounds."

"That might have made them more interesting."

"Interesting women is what got you into this mess." The woman frowned, taking me in. Still hovering. One perfectly shaped brow rose in question. "Yes? Is there a problem?"

Now it was Patrick's turn to sigh and give me a nod. He was so dreamy with his jaw and cheekbones and his everything. Real classic Hollywood handsome. Especially with his short light brown hair in artful disarray and a hint of stubble. Sometimes it was hard not to stare. Which is probably why his personality tended to scream "leave me alone."

I headed for the small bar area at the back of the restaurant to fetch the wine like a good little waitress.

"We shouldn't be discussing this here," said Angie, giving the room a disdainful sniff. Talk about judgy. I thought the raw brick walls and chunky wood tables were cool. Give or take Vinnie's collection of old black-and-white photos of Los Angeles freeways. Who knew what that was about?

Patrick slumped down even further. "I'm not going back there. I'm done with it."

"This isn't safe." Angie looked around nervously. "Let's—"

"We're fine. I've been coming here for years."

"You just got dropped from a big-budget film, Patrick," she said, exasperation in her tone. "The industry may not find you bankable right now, but I'm sure gossip about you is still selling just fine. This week at least."

A grunt from the man.

"The plan will work if you let it. Everything is organized and ready to go. It's the perfect opportunity to start rewriting the narrative in your favor." She jabbed a finger in his direction to accentuate the word "your." The woman clearly meant business, and then some.

I set the glass of wine down in front of her and returned to my place at the back of the room, polishing the silverware and restocking the salt and pepper and so on—all the jobs best performed when things were slow. And while it was nosy and wrong to listen in on other people's conversations, it wasn't my fault the room was so quiet that I could hear everything they said.

"None of them felt authentic," he said, stopping to down some more beer.

The woman snorted. "That's because none of them are."

"You know what I mean."

"When you first came to me you said you wanted to become a star, make quality films, and win an Oscar. In that order," she said. "As things are at present, you may be able to resurrect your career to some degree through the indie market. Pick up roles here and there and slowly build yourself back up. But that's going to take years and you'll likely never be in the running for the golden statuette. You can kiss that dream goodbye."

Patrick ran an agitated hand through his hair.

"You worked your ass off to get this far," she said. "Are you really going to give up now?"

"Fuck," he muttered.

"Liv is busy saving her own ass and you're unwilling to set the record straight. Not that anyone would even necessarily believe you at this point. So our options are limited." She picked up her wine, taking a delicate sip before wrinkling her nose in distaste. Since it came out of a box, that wasn't much of a surprise. She'd only asked for a glass of red; she hadn't specified quality. "I know you were hoping it would all die down, but people are still talking. And with social media how it is, this was the worst possible time to get caught up in a scandal. However, there is hope. We can still salvage things if you'd just work with us. But we need to act now."

Patrick declined to respond.

It had been all over the internet a month ago. Photos of him leaving Liv Anders's Malibu residence at the crack of dawn. And it was clearly a morning-after picture. Totally a walk of shame. He'd been all disheveled and wearing a crumpled tux. Liv being half of Hollywood's current darling couple was part of the problem. Along with Patrick and Liv's husband, Grant, having just done a movie together and supposedly being best buds. That Patrick had spent his earlier years dating a string of models and partying hard didn't help matters either. His reputation was well established. Headlines such as "Patrick the Player," "Walsh Destroys Wedded Bliss," "Friendship Failure," and "Not So Heroic Homewrecker" were everywhere. Maybe it had been a slow news week, but the amount of hate leveled at him was surprising.

Of course, there had to be more to the story. There always was. But Liv was seen weeping in a disturbingly photogenic fashion as she and her husband walked into a marriage counselor's office the next day. And the pair had been hanging off each other on the red carpet ever since. Meanwhile, Patrick's name was mud. Worse than mud. It was toxic shit.

It could all be true. He could indeed be a trash male who thought with his dick and behaved in a duplicitous and manipulative manner. I'd dated my fair share of dubious men, so it wouldn't exactly surprise me. And plenty of assholes had been publicly outed recently. Men who used their fame and power for evil.

But this all just felt more like gossip.

First up, there'd been no actual evidence that this wasn't two consenting adults doing what they wanted behind closed doors. Patrick hadn't taken any wedding vows and Liv hadn't made any accusations of mistreatment. In fact, Liv hadn't said anything at all. Patrick and Grant being best buddies, though . . . that was a hell of a betrayal. If it was true.

"Fine. I'll do it," he said, his voice rising. "But not with any of them."

"Patrick, we've been interviewing for weeks to find those three alternatives for you," she said. "One of them must be tolerable if not perfect."

"She doesn't need to be perfect. She needs to be real."

"Real?" asked Angie with some small amount of spluttering. "Give me strength. That's the last fucking thing we need right now."

The bell pinged out back. Vinnie gave me a wink and nodded to the waiting dish, Penne Ragu and Meatballs with Parmesan. It smelled divine. As the size of my ass could attest, I loved carbs and they loved me. And what was more important, jeans size or general happiness?

Vinnie took pride in his food. Pride in his restaurant. It was one of the reasons I liked working for him.

"They're all waiting. Come back to the office," said Angie as I reentered the room.

"No."

"Patrick, how the hell else are you going to find someone? If word of what we were doing got out . . ."

"That's not going to happen."

The woman looked to heaven, but no help was forthcoming. "If you won't choose one of them, then who?"

"I don't know," he growled.

As stealthily as possible, I set the meal down in front of him. Invisibility was an art form. One I didn't always excel at when he was around. It's not my fault. Attractive men make me nervous. So of course my fingers fumbled over the silverware and the fork clattered loudly to the table.

"Her," he said, staring right at me. Possibly the only time we'd made direct eye contact. It was like looking into the sun. I was all but blinded. The man was just too much.

"What?!" Angie shrieked.

I froze. He couldn't be referring to me. Not unless it was in the context of a "you are totally clumsy and not getting a tip today" sort of thing.

"You cannot be serious," Angie all but spluttered, looking me over, her eyes wide as twin moons. "She's so . . . average."

"Yeah," he agreed with enthusiasm.

Wow, harsh. I was pretty in my own way. Beige skin and long, wavy blond hair. A freckle or two on my face. As for my body, not everyone in this city had to be stick thin. But whatever. The important thing was, I was a nice person. Most of the time. And I was kind. Or at least, I tried to be. Personal growth can be tricky.

"Enjoy your meal," I said with a frown on my face.

"Sit down a minute." Patrick gestured to the space beside him in the booth. "Please."

Instead, I crossed my arms.

"I want to talk to you about a job opportunity."

Angie made a strangled noise.

"I have a job," I said. "Actually, I have two."

"What's your name?" he asked.

"You've got to be joking," hissed Angie. "They'll never believe it."

"Norah," I said.

"Hey, Norah. I'm Patrick."

"I know," I deadpanned.

He almost smiled. There was a definite twitch of the lips. For someone whose charm-laden devil-may-care grin had graced billboards all over the country, he sure knew how to keep that sucker under wraps. "How'd you like to make some serious money?"

"Don't say another word until she's signed an NDA." With a hand clutched to her chest, Angie appeared to be either hyperventilating or having a heart attack. "I mean it!"

Patrick just sighed. "Angie, relax. I've been coming in here for years and she's never once put anything on social media or taken a creeper shot. I bet you haven't told a soul about me, have you, Norah?"

So I respected his privacy. So sue me. I also kind of liked hearing him say my name. Him just knowing it was a thrill. Definite weakness of the knees. "You seem to enjoy the anonymity."

"Even stopped that girl from asking me for an autograph."

"The owner's daughter," I said. "She's still not talking to me."

Another almost-smile. There was definite amusement in his pretty blue eyes.

Angie downed the last of her boxed wine in one large gulp.

Patrick and I stared at each other like it was a contest. Who would dare look away first? Me, apparently.

"What's the job?" I asked.

"I'd need you full time for a couple of months," he said.

"A year, and live-in," corrected Angie.

Patrick cringed. "Six months and live-in. No more."

With a wave of her fingers, Angie relented.

I cleared my throat. "Um, doing what, exactly? Being your gofer or an assistant or something? Or do you need like a house-keeper or a cleaner?"

"No," he said, calm as can be. "I want you to be my fake girlfriend."

Get *Fake* from your favorite online retailer today!

Purchase Kylie Scott's Other Books

Pause

Fake

The Rich Boy

Love Under Quarantine

Repeat

Lies

It Seemed Like a Good Idea at the Time

Trust

THE DIVE BAR SERIES
Dirty

Twist

Chaser

THE STAGE DIVE SERIES
Lick

Play

Lead

Deep

Strong: A Stage Dive Novella

THE FLESH SERIES
Flesh

Skin

Flesh Series Novellas

Heart's a Mess

Colonist's Wife

About

KYLIE SCOTT

Kylie is a *New York Times*, *Wall Street Journal*, and *USA Today* bestselling, Audie Award winning author. She has sold over 2,000,000 books and was voted Australian Romance Writer of the year, 2013, 2014, 2018, & 2019, by the Australian Romance Reader's Association. Her books have been translated into fourteen different languages. She is based in Queensland, Australia.

www.kyliescott.com
Facebook: www.facebook.com/kyliescottwriter
Twitter: twitter.com/KylieScottbooks
Instagram: www.instagram.com/kylie_scott_books
Pinterest: www.pinterest.com/kyliescottbooks
BookBub: www.bookbub.com/authors/kylie-scott

**To learn about exclusive content, my upcoming releases and giveaways, join my newsletter:
https://kyliescott.com/subscribe**